The Legend of Dogwood Mountain

JOHN GARRISON

ISBN 979-8-89243-405-8 (paperback)
ISBN 979-8-89243-406-5 (digital)

Copyright © 2024 by John Garrison

All rights reserved. No part of this publication may be reproduced, distributed, or transmitted in any form or by any means, including photocopying, recording, or other electronic or mechanical methods without the prior written permission of the publisher. For permission requests, solicit the publisher via the address below.

Christian Faith Publishing
832 Park Avenue
Meadville, PA 16335
www.christianfaithpublishing.com

Printed in the United States of America

Chapter 1

My name is Seth Adams. I grew up on a small ten-acre farm about fifty miles south of Memphis, Tennessee. It was near a small coal-mining town called Brookside. My father was a coal miner, and my mother worked in the school lunchroom kitchen. I was an only child and spent a lot of time working on the farm. We grew most of the food we ate, and the food we didn't need, my mother would sell and save the money to send me to college. She wanted me to grow up and be a schoolteacher. I was not really happy with that idea, but I never told her that. I was always big for my age. When I was sixteen years old, I was 6'1" and weighed 197 lb. I spent a lot of time playing sports. John Baker was a good friend of mine, and growing up together, we played a lot of football in the backyard. When we went in the tenth grade at school, the coach asked both of us to join the football team. After spring practice training, the coach said John and I were the two best players he had ever seen. John played quarterback, and I was a wide receiver. We practiced together a lot and could almost read each other's mind. We won state championships all three years we played in high school. After we finished high school, we were given full scholarships to play at Memphis State University. While attending the university, John decided he wanted to study real estate. I was in charge of the college newspaper and decided that was what I wanted to do. After we graduated, John went to work for a real estate company, and I went to work for a newspaper company. The *Memphis Star* was a small newspaper. There was not a lot to write about in Memphis, but I kept thinking, maybe one day a good story would come my way. I heard John was doing really well in the real estate business, and I was just barely getting by. I left to go to work this morning, and I was running late as usual. When I got to the office and walked in, Jane was sitting at her front desk and said, "Good morning, Seth. Looks like you're running late again! Mr. Jones wants to see you in his office."

"Thank you, Jane. That's what I needed to hear this morning," and I walked over to my desk, set my briefcase down, and headed for Mr. Jones's office.

I knocked on his door and walked in and said, "Good morning, boss."

He was leaning back and, in his chair, smoking a big cigar and said, "Come in, Seth. Take a seat. There's something I need to talk to you about, son. Seth, it's been a long time since you've written anything that the people want to read about. Now here is what I want to talk to you about: I want you to go to your desk, get your laptop and your camera and maybe your tape recorder, and go out and find a good story to write about. Don't come back until you have something good to print in the paper."

"Yes, sir boss, I'll get started right away."

I got up and left his office and walked down the hallway to my desk, gathered all my belongings, and headed to the front door. I said goodbye to everyone in the office as I went out the door and headed to my car. On the way to my car, I got the feeling that maybe I was getting fired. I kept thinking maybe I would find that good story and redeem myself. I got in my car and drove out of the parking lot, not really knowing where I was going or what I was going to do. As I was driving down the street, I noticed a half-eaten bag of popcorn in the seat, and I thought, *Well, I might just go down to the park and feed the pigeons that bag of popcorn. When* I got to the park, I sat down on the bench and started feeding the pigeons, and my cell phone started ringing. "Hello, this is Seth."

"Hello, Seth, this is John. How are you doing, buddy?"

"Hey, John, I'm doing great. Haven't seen or heard from you in a while? How are you doing?"

"I'm doing fine, Seth. If you're not really busy, how about riding down to Nashville with me this afternoon? I've got to sign some papers on a real estate deal, and I have to be there at 5:00 to sign the papers. I was thinking, if we left at noon today, we could be there by 3:30. That would give me enough time to get a room and meet my 5:00 appointment. I know a lady there that owns a small hotel and bar, and we can spend the night and head back tomorrow morning."

"That sounds great, John. I will go to my apartment to get a few things, and you can pick me up there at noon. I'll send you the address."

"Okay, Seth. I'll pick you up at noon."

I said bye to John and headed for my apartment. I got to the apartment, went in, and started packing a few clothes.

I kept thinking, *Maybe this is my big chance to find a good story. There's always a lot of things going on in Nashville, and maybe I'll find something good to write about.*

John arrived about 12:05, and we left Memphis and headed to Nashville.

On the way to Nashville, we talked a lot about the college days and all the fun we had while we were there. We arrived in Nashville about 3:45 and got to the Blue Moon Hotel, checked in, and went up to our rooms. We got settled in. After a while, John and I met downstairs in the lobby. John said he had to leave and go to get some paper signed and would meet up with me later. After John left, I decided to sit down in the bar until he got back. I sat down, and the bartender asked me what I would like to drink. I ordered a Coke. The bartender said, "Coke is not going to get you talking very much. You must not be from around here."

"No, I'm not. I'm a newspaper writer from Memphis. I thought, since I was in Nashville, I might find a good story to write about. My name is Seth Adams. What is your name?"

"My name is Becky, Seth. I own this hotel and bar. A good friend of mine helped me purchase it years ago. Now it would be a good story for you to write about. His name is Rusty Wilson."

"I have heard about a man with that name Becky. He is one of the richest and most powerful men in America."

"Yes, he is, Seth. And how he got there would be one of the best stories you could ever write about. Rusty and I grew up in a little town called Indian Springs, Tennessee. I have a lot of things to do this afternoon, but if you want to know more about Rusty, meet me back here in the morning at 8:00, and I will tell you a lot about him."

"I'll be here, Becky, and talk to you in the morning."

Becky left, and I sat at the bar and waited for John to return. When he arrived, I told him about Becky and how she was going to give me a good story to write about.

"Well, Seth, Becky and I have been good friends for a long time, and whatever she tells you will be the truth."

John and I spent the afternoon talking, and the next morning, he got ready to go back to Memphis. I told him I was going to stay in Nashville and would see him later. John left, and I went to the dining room and waited for Becky to come down. She'll finally arrive, and I invited her to have breakfast with me. We talked for a while. And after we finished breakfast, she invited me to her office.

We went into her office, and she said, "Sit down, Seth, and I will tell you all about Rusty."

I spent the next four days with Becky, listening to all the stories she told me about Rusty and how she and all her friends grew up there. Indian Springs was a small town at that time, and she told me how growing up there was very special.

I told Becky I appreciate all the information she gave me, and I would be back in town again. I got my things together and left the hotel and rented a car. I decided to drive to Indian Springs and do some more research on Rusty Wilson. As I left Nashville, I called my boss and told him about the story I was going to write, and I would get in touch with him as soon as I could. I got to the interstate and headed north to Indian Springs. It was about a four-hour drive from Nashville. When I arrived in town, I rented a room not too far from the house that Rusty grew up in. I got settled in the room and decided to start my research on Rusty and his family. I left and went down to the hall of records in the courthouse and started my research.

Here is what I found out about Rusty and his family: In 1897, Edward Wilson's wife died, and he decided to leave Savannah Georgia with his six-year-old son named Carl Wilson. Edward was a cabinetmaker by trade, and he decided to take his son west, looking for a new place to build a home. They came to a valley called Indian Springs. The town was settled in the early 1700s. The valley was once the home of the Native American Indians. There were about 1,500 Indians that lived there. When the white settlers started moving in the valley, they were having problems with the Indians, and the government decided to move the Indians to a reservation in Oklahoma. A small band of Indians did not want to leave, so they moved up into the mountains nearby. As time went by, this small band of Indians would travel at night, down in the valley, and take whatever food they could find to survive in the mountains. A lot of people in the valley began to complain about losing their food, and the men in the valley decided to get rid of the problem. They waited for the Indians to come down one night and followed them up into the mountains. They waited several hours for the Indians to settle down in their campsite. Once they were asleep, the men started firing into the campsite and killed all thirteen of the Indians.

They buried them under piles of rocks at their campsite. Now that the Indians were gone, they felt like their town would be safe again. More and more White people begin moving into the valley. When Edward Wilson moved into the valley, he put a claim on 485 acres of land and got a deed recorded in the land office. The land was covered with beautiful hardwood trees and giant pine trees. Edward was not only a good cabinetmaker but also a good carpenter.

He told his son, "Carl, this is where we're going to build our new home. All we need now is a one-man sawmill and we can start building our home. Edward traveled all over the valley looking for a sawmill." He found one that was for sale for $100. Edward offered him $50 and one of his mules for the Sawmill. The man decided to take the deal, and now Edward had all that he needed to get his house started. They set the sawmill up and got started, cutting the timber they needed for their house.

Chapter 2

Edward had seen a house in Savannah, Georgia, that he loved and decided to build one just like it. It took four years to build the house in which Edward and Carl lived. It was one of the most beautiful houses in the valley. They built their cabinet shop in the back of the house and began to build cabinets and houses for people moving into the valley. After years went by, Carl grew up and learned how to build cabinets and houses as good as his father. Carl was nineteen years old when his father, Edward, got pneumonia and died. Edward was buried in a small cemetery right outside of town. Two years had passed since Edward had died, and Carl was working, doing some repair work on a doctor's house, when he met a young lady, whose name was Martha Smith. They dated for about two years and got married.

Two years later, they had a son and named him James. When James was seventeen years old, his mother became sick and died. After Martha died, Carl seemed to lose interest in everything around him. He would spend most of his time sitting on the riverbank, trying to find something to hold on to. James kept telling his father that things would get better. When James turned twenty, he met a lady named Mary, and they got married and had a son named Rusty. As soon as Rusty was born, Carl started getting better. Carl was getting really attached to Rusty, and he told James, "Someday this boy is going to be somebody special in this world!"

As time went by, Rusty would follow his grandfather around all over the cabinet shop. Carl told James, "Rusty may turn out to be a better cabinet builder than myself."

James replied, "His mother may have better plans for him."

Rusty was about five years old when James and Mary decided they would go into business for themselves. They found a small vacant lot downtown and opened up a hardware store. They named the story J&M Hardware. As time went by, the store began doing a lot of business and became one of the biggest hardware stores in town. James and Mary would spend most of their time working there. Rusty started school, and every afternoon, when he got home, you would find him out in the cabinet shop, working with his grandfather.

Carl told James, "Rusty is a real smart kid, and someday he will make a good cabinetmaker."

"I don't want Rusty to be a cabinetmaker, Dad, when he finishes school. I want him to go to college. I would like for him to go to Georgia Tech and learn to be an engineer."

"Well, that will be good, James, if that's what the boy wants to do." What happened next would change Rusty's life forever.

Early that morning, James and Mary came down and walked into the kitchen where Carl was putting on the coffeepot.

Carl asked James, "What are you doing down here this early in the morning?"

James replied, "Mary and I are going to Kentucky this morning to buy some materials from another hardware store that's going out of business. They have a lot of materials that we can get real cheap and make good money off of. We're leaving our hardware store as soon as we can get to the big truck and get ready to go."

"Where is the store you're talking about, James?"

"It's in a little town just across the border in Kentucky. If you don't mind, Dad, will you make sure Rusty gets off to school on time?"

"Don't worry about Rusty, James. I'll make sure he makes it to school. You all go ahead and do what you have to do."

James and Mary left, and Carl started making breakfast. Carl went upstairs and told Rusty to get up and get ready for school. He had breakfast waiting for him.

About twenty minutes later, Rusty came running down the stairs and sat down to eat his breakfast. "Where's Mom and Dad, Grandpa?"

"They left early this morning, Rusty, going to Kentucky to buy some materials for the hardware store. They should be back by the time you get back from school."

Carl looked out the window and saw Becky standing by the gate, waiting on Rusty. "Becky's waiting on you, Rusty, so hurry up!"

Rusty gathered up his books and headed out the door.

Becky yelled, "Hurry up, Rusty! We're going to be late for school."

Rusty and Becky headed off to school, laughing and cutting up, like all nine-year-old kids do. After cleaning the kitchen up, Carl went out to his cabinet shop to do some work. About 11:00, Carl decided to take a break and walk back to his house. He went into the kitchen, got a glass of water, and walked out on the front porch and sat down in his favorite rocking chair. He had been sitting there for about ten minutes when the police car pulled up in the front of the house. It was an old friend, Paul Cooper, the police chief of Indian Springs. Paul got out of his car and walked up to the sidewalk to where Carl was sitting.

Carl said, "Come on up. Paul. Sit down, and we'll talk a while."

"Carl, I don't have time for a break. I need you to come downtown with me. I've got some bad news to tell you. It's about James and Mary."

"What do you mean bad news, Paul?"

"Come and get in the car with me, Carl, and I will tell you on the way downtown."

Carl got in the car with Paul, and they headed downtown.

"It's James and Mary, Carl, who have been killed in an accident just across the state line in Kentucky. Their bodies were brought here to the morgue in town. I have come to get you so you can identify the bodies."

Carl sat there in shock; he couldn't believe what he was hearing. "No, this can't be true, Paul."

"I'm sorry, Carl, for bringing you this bad news. I know how hard it's going to be on you, but it's going to be even harder on that boy you have at home. You're not only going to have to be strong for yourself but also for Rusty. When Rusty hears this, it's going to break his little heart."

They arrived at the morgue, and Carl went in and then identified James's and Mary's bodies. After seeing their bodies, Carl broke down and started crying. Paul took him off to the side of the room and talked to him.

"You're going to have to be strong, Carl. That little boy is going to need you more than ever. We've been friends for a long time, Carl, and I will do anything I can to help you get through this."

They sat there for about an hour talking, and Paul said, "Let me take you home."

When Paul got Carl home, they walked up the sidewalk to the front porch. Carl walked up the steps. And when he got to the top, he sat down.

"Rusty will be getting home from school in a few minutes. Would you like for me to stay and help you talk to him?"

"No, Paul. I appreciate what you've done for me. I will have to do this on my own. I really don't know what I'm going to have to say to the boy. I know this will shatter his world."

"Well, if you need me, Carl, call me, and I'll be right over."

"Thank you, Paul."

Paul walked down the sidewalk and got in his car and started leaving. Carl sat there on the top step, wondering what he was going to say to Rusty. *How do you tell a youngster that his parents have been killed? What will you say to him to make him understand?* Carl was sitting there, waiting for Rusty to come home, and he didn't have to wait long. He could see Rusty and Becky walking down the street. They were talking and laughing and carrying on like two happy kids should be doing.

Becky said, "Look, Rusty, there's a police car leaving the front of your house."

"Yes, I see that it must be Mr. Paul. He's a good friend of my grandpa's."

When they reached the front gate, Becky said, "Look, Rusty, there's your grandpa sitting on the top step!"

"Yes, he's probably been working out in the shop, and he's now sitting there, taking a break."

"Well, bye, Rusty. I'll see you in the morning."

"Okay, Becky, I'll see you later."

Rusty walked up to the front porch steps, and his grandpa sat there with tears running down his face.

Rusty looked at him and said, "What's the matter, Grandpa? Why are you crying?"

His grandpa looked up at him and said, "Sit down here beside me, Rusty. I have some bad news to tell you. It's going to be really hard, and you have to be strong for what I'm about to tell you."

"What's the matter, Grandpa?"

"Your mom and dad are not coming home!"

"What do you mean, Grandpa? They're not coming home?"

"Rusty, your mom and dad have been killed in a car wreck!"

"No, Grandpa, this can't be true."

Rusty jumped up from the steps into the house, calling for his mother and father. "Mom, where are you?" He ran through the house upstairs and downstairs, looking everywhere for his mom and dad, but they were nowhere to be found. Rusty ran out the back door, screaming for his parents, and started running down the street, crying and running, not knowing where he was going. Rusty's grandpa tried to catch up with him, but he was too late. Rusty ran out of sight down the street. Rusty's grandpa ran back and got in his truck and started down the street, looking for Rusty. He drove all over town and could not find him.

Grandpa called his friend Paul and asked him to help find Rusty. The police started looking all over town for Rusty. Later that afternoon, just before dark, the police officer found Rusty sitting on the steps at the football stadium. He walked up to Rusty and said, "I've got to take you home now. Your grandpa needs you real bad."

Rusty didn't say anything, just walked away with the police officer with his head down. The police officer took Rusty to the front door and turned him over to his grandfather. Carl took Rusty into the house and sat him down with him and started talking to him about how they had to stick together and get through this. Rusty sat there and did not say anything with his head down, tears coming out of his eyes. "Grandpa, why did this happen to Mom and Dad?"

"I don't know how things happen in life that we just don't understand. We have to take care of each other now."

Grandpa and Rusty sat there for several hours and talked to each other, trying to find some sense in all this. Rusty looked at his grandpa and said, "I'm going to bed now, Grandpa. I'll see you in the morning."

Rusty gave his grandpa a big hug and walked up the stairs to his room. The next morning, Carl was waiting for Rusty to get up when he heard a knock on the door. He opened the door, and Becky was standing there.

"I heard about Rusty's parents, and I guess he's not going to school today?"

"No, Becky, he won't be going to school for a few days now. I will tell him you came by."

"Thank you, Mr. Wilson. I'm sorry for your loss."

Becky turned and walked away, going down the steps and heading to school. Carl received several phone calls from people offering to help him and Rusty. Later on that morning, Rusty walked down from the upstairs and entered the kitchen, where his grandfather was sitting.

"What do we do now, Grandpa?"

"It's going to take us a while for us to get through this, Rusty. Right now we have to go downtown and make some arrangements."

The next two days seemed like a hundred years for Rusty while they were getting ready to bury his mother and dad. On the third day, they had the funeral for James and Mary. They buried them next to his great-grandfather. It seemed like the whole town showed up for the funeral that day. You had barely room to walk around. It was one of the saddest days in the history of Indian Springs, Tennessee. After the funeral was over, Rusty and his grandfather went back home. Rusty asked his grandfather, "What am I going to do now, Grandpa?"

"All I can tell you, son, is you're going to grow up and be a good and strong man like your parents wanted you to be. It's going to take us a while to get over this, but we will see better days."

Two weeks went by, and Rusty was back in school. He came home one day from school, and his grandpa said, "Come in here. I want to talk to you." Rusty's Grandpa walked over to the fireplace and picked up the guitar. "This guitar belongs to your dad. I taught him how to play it, and now I'm going to teach you."

Rusty walked over to his grandpa and said, "Do you think I can learn how to play the guitar?"

"Sure you can, Rusty! You can learn anything you want to if you set your mind to do it."

Every day, Carl would work in his cabinet shop, and in the afternoons, when Rusty got home from school, he would sit down and teach him how to play the guitar. Rusty told Becky, "My grandpa is teaching me how to play the guitar."

"Well, you learn how to play the guitar, Rusty, and I will learn how to sing."

As time passed, Rusty began to get back just doing some of the things he enjoyed doing. When school was out in the summer, Rusty would spend time in the cabinet shop, helping his grandfather. He was learning how to build cabinets at an early age. Rusty told his grandfather, when he graduated from high school, he wanted to start his own construction company."

"Well, that's okay, Rusty, but don't forget what your father wanted. He wanted you to go to college and study engineering."

"I know, Grandpa, but I don't think that's what I want to do."

"Well, you still have several years of school left, and there's plenty of time to think about that. Six years have passed, and Rusty was in the tenth grade of school and decided to get together with some of his friends and form a little band. Rusty could play the guitar really good, and three of his buddies were also good guitar players and drummers. Becky joined the group and would be doing the singing. Everyone agreed that Becky had a good voice and could be a great singer one day. Becky told Rusty, 'When I graduate from high school, I plan to move to Nashville and sing for a living.'"

"That sounds like a great plan, Becky. You are a good singer."

As time passed, Rusty learned more and more about building cabinets and construction work. He would be graduating from high school in a few months and had big plans for him and his grandfather to work in the construction business.

Chapter 3

Four months had passed, and Rusty was three days from graduating from high school. He was so excited about finishing school. Now he could get his own construction business going.

Becky asked, "Rusty, what are you going to name your construction company?"

He said, "The name will be Wilson Construction Company. Before I'm finished, I will be heard worldwide."

"That sounds so exciting, Rusty. I know you will make your dream come true."

"What about you, Becky? What are you going to do when you graduate?"

"I want to be a singer, Rusty. I plan to move to Nashville. I have a cousin there that works in a nightclub. She says she can get me a job there, and I hope to start singing."

"Well, Becky, I think you will do good in Nashville. Maybe one day I can come down and hear you sing."

"I would love for you to do that, Rusty."

"Rusty and Becky were walking home from school and decided to go over and sit down on the football bleachers and talk. They had been sitting there for about twenty minutes when they saw a police car pull up in front of the stadium. The police officer was Mr. Paul, a good friend of Rusty's grandfather. Mr. Paul walked up to Rusty and said, "Rusty, you need to come with me to the hospital. Your grandfather is there, and he is very ill."

Rusty told Becky he would see her later and got in the car with Officer Paul, and they drove down to the hospital. Officer Paul took

THE LEGEND OF DOGWOOD MOUNTAIN

Rusty into the emergency room, where they had his grandfather. When he walked into the room where his grandfather was lying, he saw all these wires and tubes hooked up to his grandfather. Rusty told the doctor who he was, and the doctor told him that his grandfather had a massive heart attack.

"We're doing all we can for him, but it's not looking good."

Rusty asked the doctor if he could walk over and talk to his grandfather.

"You can walk over there, but he's not able to talk, Rusty."

Rusty walked over to his grandfather and said, "Here I am, Grandpa."

His grandfather opened his eyes and raised his hand up, and Rusty took his hand. As Rusty stood there, holding his grandfather's hand, the warning lights started flashing, and the emergency blue code came on. The doctors told Rusty he would have to leave the room.

Rusty turned his grandfather's hand loose and walked out of the room. Several people were running in and out of the room. Officer Paul told Rusty to come over and sit down on the bench next to him. After about twenty minutes, the doctors came out and told Rusty that his grandfather had died.

Rusty couldn't believe what he was hearing. His whole world had been shattered again. He sat down on the bench and began to cry.

Officer Paul put his arm around Rusty and said, "I'm sorry for your loss, Rusty. I'm here for you, and I will do anything I can to make this a little easier on you."

The doctor came back out and told Rusty, "If you want to see him again, you can go in the room now."

Rusty and Officer Paul got up and walked back into the room where his grandfather was. Rusty stood there a few minutes, looking at his grandfather and thinking to himself, *This can't be true.*

Officer Paul looked at Rusty and said, "Come on, son, let me take you home."

Officer Paul took Rusty home, and when he got there, Officer Paul sat down and told Rusty he would do all he could to help him make arrangements for his grandfather. Officer Paul stayed there for several hours, talking to Rusty and telling him what they were going to have to do. He told Rusty he would be back tomorrow morning to pick him up, and they would go downtown to take care of his grandfather.

"Is there anything I can do for you before I leave, Rusty?"

"No, sir, I will be okay, and I will see you tomorrow."

The next day, Officer Paul picked up Rusty, and they went down to the funeral home and made all the arrangements for his grandfather. The next two days, Rusty spent all his time at home. Becky and a lot of his friends came by and talked with him. They all told him how sorry they were for his loss. The next day, they had the funeral for his grandfather. That afternoon, Rusty's grandfather was buried in the cemetery plot next to Rusty's mother and father. The next few days, Rusty kept to himself. Becky came by to see Rusty. She asked him why he missed graduation. He told her the principal said he could pick up his diploma anytime he was ready. He told Becky, "My grandfather had a cabinet job that he never finished, and he was going to start to work on it the next day. I'm going to finish the job and start my construction company. That is what my grandpa would want me to do."

"I'm leaving Friday and going to Nashville, Rusty."

"That's a good thing, Becky. You need to follow your dream. I know you will do good in Nashville. Call me when you have a chance, and let me know how things are going."

"I will, Rusty, and I want you to know that I will be missing you very much."

Becky gave Rusty a big hug and walked away. Rusty sat there on the porch and watched Becky drive away. He was thinking about all the good times that he and Becky had growing up. The next three weeks, Rusty spent in the cabinet shop, finishing up the job that his grandfather had started. He was working on the cabinets when he got a phone call from his grandfather's lawyer. He asked Rusty to come down to his office the next day. The next day, Rusty drove down to the lawyer's office. When Rusty walked into the office, his friend, Officer Paul, was sitting there. The attorney, Mr. Davis, asked

Rusty, "I hope you don't mind Police Chief Paul being here. We have to have a witness on some of the paperwork that you have to sign."

"No, I don't mind. Mr. Davis. Mr. Paul has been a good friend to me and my family for a long time."

"We are here to read your grandfather's will. Your grandfather's will states that everything he owns, he is leaving to you, Rusty Wilson. Your grandfather has left you 840 acres and the house that is located on the property. The money in the bank he left has a grand total of two million. Most of that money came from the trucking company who had killed your parents. Some of the money came from the sale of the hardware store."

Rusty couldn't believe that his grandfather had left him so much money. Their lawyer looked at Rusty and said, "He also left a note here for you."

Rusty got the note and opened it up and started reading it. It said, "Rusty, you have always been my pride and joy, and now you have the money to build that construction company that you've always talked about. I never knew when this day might come, but I want to wish you all the luck and happiness you can have in your life. Goodbye, my son. I love you dearly."

Rusty said, "I hope I can grow up and be as good of a man as my grandpa was." Rusty signed all the paperwork that was needed and thank the attorney for his work. Rusty and Officer Paul left the attorney's office. When they reached the outside, Officer Paul told Rusty, "You have everything you need now to be anything you want to be."

Rusty told Officer Paul, "I'm going to build the biggest construction company this state has ever seen. I'm going to make my parents and my grandparents proud of me."

"I know you will, Rusty. And if you ever need any help, please call me."

"Thank you, Mr. Paul. I appreciate everything you have done for me. And if there's anything I can ever do for you, please let me know." Rusty thanked Officer Paul for all he had done and left to go back to his home. When he got home, he started making plans to get his construction business started.

Chapter 4

The next day, Rusty went down to the courthouse to get his license to start his construction company. After he got his license, he started looking for people to work for him. He put "Help Wanted" signs up at the hardware store and various places all over town. Everyone in Indian Springs knew Rusty and his grandfather. He was too soon to have more business work than he could do. Rusty visited several businesses in town. He stopped at the hardware store and the lumber company and made many other stops at different businesses and told them he would be buying materials as he needed for his company. Rusty was getting a lot of calls from the "Help Wanted" signs he put out. He invited them to come by his cabinet shop, where he would interview them. After several days of interviews, he had two men working in the cabinet shop and three working in the remodeling part of his business. Rusty had been using the cabinet shop as his office, and one day he decided he would go downtown and find a place to make a new office.

He came up on a vacant lot that used to be a used car lot. There was a small building on the lot he could use for an office and a building, and in the back he could use for storage. The man who owned the used car lot was named Mr. Massey. Rusty called him and asked if he was willing to sell the place. Mr. Massey agreed to come down and meet with Rusty at the car lot and talk about selling it. Mr. Massey asked Rusty what he had planned to do with the property. Rusty told him he was going to make a construction office on the property.

"I've heard about you, Rusty. Are you Carl Wilson's grandson?"

"Yes, I am."

"I knew your grandfather, and he was a fine man. Everyone in town knew he was a man of his word."

"I appreciate all the kind words you're saying about my grandfather. He was a very great man, and I loved him more than anyone will ever know. Are you interested in selling this property, Mr. Massey?"

"Yes, I thought about selling the property."

"What are you asking for the property, sir?"

"I'll take $25,000 for the car lot, but I also have a cabin in Dogwood Mountain that I want to sell. If you want the car lot, you have to buy the cabin also. I want $5,000 for the cabin."

"I'm willing to pay the $25,000 for the car lot, Mr. Massey, but I'm not sure about the cabin."

"Well, Rusty, I'm going to sell the car lot, and the cabin in a package deal. If you want them, you'll have to buy both of them. It's a really nice cabin, and I think you'll be very surprised at how well it looks, Rusty."

"Okay, Mr. Massey, I will go up and look at the cabin with you."

"I'll meet you here tomorrow morning at nine o'clock, Rusty, and will drive up and have a look."

"Okay, Mr. Massey, I'll see you here in the morning."

The next morning, they met and drove up into the mountains to see the cabin. It was about a one-hour drive from Indian Springs to where the cabin was located in the mountains. It was a beautiful old cabin built by Mr. Massey's grandfather.

"How much land goes with the cabin, Mr. Massey?"

"The cabin sits on a five-acre tract of land, Rusty."

They walked all around the cabin and went outside. Rusty could tell the cabin was well constructed and very well taken care of.

"Come walk with me down to the edge of the bluff. I want to show you something, Rusty."

They walk down the hill, about a hundred yards to the edge, and Mr. Massey said, "Look down there, Rusty." There was about a hundred-foot drop-off down to a ledge, where there was a small stream of water coming out of the side of the mountain. "You see that trail along the edge down there? That's where deer come down and drink every afternoon. It's a beautiful sight watching the deer come and go from the pool of water."

"Yes, Mr. Massey, I would love to see that. I really like what I've already seen so far. I think this place is well worth what you're asking for at, Mr. Massey. I like the car lot, and I like what I've seen here. I would very much like to buy this and the car lot from you. We can go back to the valley, and I will get the money to pay you for the two pieces of property."

"There's one more thing I want to show you, Rusty. Come with me."

Rusty started walking up the hill with Mr. Massey. They walked about a quarter of a mile up the road, and there was a small trail leading out into the woods. They walked about a hundred yards off the road, and there was a pile of rocks scattered all around a small area.

"What are these rocks doing here, Mr. Massey?"

"This is an old Indian burial ground. There is a story that my father's grandfather told him, and my father told me. There was a small group of Indians killed here by some of the White settlers. My father said this piece of property here was a sacred ground. I don't know if you believe in spirits, Rusty, but I do believe there are spirits living here."

"Well, Mr. Massey, that's an interesting story, but I'm not sure if I believe in spirits that would be living here."

"Well, I've never seen or heard of any myself, but you never know. If there are spirits here, Mr. Massey, I'm not afraid of them."

"Neither am I, Rusty. But if you buy this property, you will own the burial ground."

Rusty and Mr. Massey left for the valley, and when they got there, Rusty got the money and paid Mr. Massey for the two pieces of property. The next day, Rusty started making plans to open up his office there at the used car lot. Rusty carried two of his helpers to the car lot and started cleaning the building, getting ready to open up his office. The building had one large room and one small room. The bathroom is located at the end of the building. Rusty spent several days repairing the inside of the building and getting it to look almost new. He brought in a desk for each of the rooms in the building. He installed filing cabinets for all his paperwork.

He brought all the files from the cabinet shop down to the new office. Now all he needed was a secretary. He ran an ad in the small-town paper, asking for someone to be a secretary for his business. The next day, a young lady came by and applied for the job.

"Hello, Rusty. My name is Sally Rivers. Do you remember me in high school?"

"Of course, I do, Sally. You and Becky were good friends in school. Are you here to apply for the secretary job?"

"Yes, Rusty, I've been going to night school, studying secretarial work, and I would like to apply for the job, working for you."

"Well, I need someone immediately. Are you ready to go to work?"

"Yes, I am, Rusty. I'm ready whenever you are."

"Well, Sally, you've got the job. Let me show you around the office."

Rusty spent the rest of the day showing Sally all the things she would be required to do.

"The company is getting bigger, and there are a lot of people coming in and filling out applications for jobs. You will take their applications and do a background check on each one of them. Everyone that works for the company will meet here every Monday morning at seven o'clock to get their weekly schedule. I will get with you, Sally, every Friday and make sure their schedules are ready for Monday morning."

"I appreciate the job, Rusty, and I promise to do the best I can for the company."

"I'm sure you will do fine, Sally, and I hope you enjoy working for the company."

Sally had been working for about two weeks when two men came into the office, looking for a job. She gave them the applications to fill out, and they would be interviewed by the owner as soon as they completed the applications. After they finished the applications, Sally called Rusty and told him that she had two men in the office, looking for a job. Rusty left the job he was on and came to the office to meet with the two men. Sally introduced the two men to Rusty.

"This is Mark Johnson, and his brother, Jesse. This is Rusty Wilson, the owner of the company."

"I'm pleased to meet you, Mark and Jesse. I remember you from my high school days. I was in the tenth grade, and, Mark, you were in the twelfth grade."

"I remember you too, Rusty. You were in the tenth grade with my brother Jesse."

Rusty started looking over the application. "I see here, you worked for Roger Kelly's construction company."

"That's true, Rusty. Jesse and I both worked for him and decided to quit because we didn't like the way he wanted the jobs done. He wanted us to do shoddy work, and we didn't like that. We heard you had a good reputation for doing quality work, and that's what we want to do."

"Well, I appreciate that, Mark, and that's what I expect from all of my employees." Rusty talked to Mark and Jesse for about an hour, and he was really pleased with the attitude about the work. "Come to the office in the morning at seven o'clock, and I will get you started on the jobs that I have lined up."

Mark and Jesse left that afternoon and were really happy about the new job they were about to work for. The next morning, Rusty carried Mark and Jesse to one of his jobsites. He gave them instructions on what he wanted them to do, and he would come back later and see how things were going. Everything was going good on all the jobs Rusty had going, and after two weeks on the job, Mark and Jesse were doing such a good job. Rusty put them in charge of running two separate jobs. Rusty told Sally, "I think Mark and Jesse may be the two best men we have working with. I think my company is going on its way to the top."

"I think you're right. The rest of your company is getting bigger and better every day."

Chapter 5

One Saturday morning, Rusty decided to ride up into the mountain and visit the cabin he had purchased. On the way up the mountain, all the dogwood trees were in full bloom. They were beautiful white blossoms shining in the sunlight. Rusty was thinking to himself, *I can see now why they call this Dogwood Mountain.* It was a real sight to behold and he was so glad he had bought the cabin.

When he reached the cabin, he got out of his truck, and he could hear a sound coming from the Indian burial ground. He decided to walk up to the burial ground and see what the sound was. When he got there, the sound was gone. He saw a man walking away from the side, and he asked him who he was. The man turned and looked at Rusty and said, "My name is Gus. Who are you?"

"My name is Rusty Wilson. I own this property. What are you doing here?"

"Well, Mr. Wilson, I come here on occasion to visit the Indian burial ground. I think there's something special about this place, and I come down here every chance I get."

"Where are you from, Gus?"

"I live just a little ways up the mountain."

"If you like looking at the burial site, Gus, why don't you do something about cleaning it up and making it look a little better?"

"I would love to do that, Mr. Wilson. But what can I do?"

"Well, next weekend I will come up here and bring some tools, and we can clean this place up. Stack the rocks up, and make the grave look a little better."

"That would be very nice, Mr. Wilson. I think the spirits here will love that." He just turned and started walking away and said, "I'll be back next week, Mr. Wilson."

"Good. I will see you then, Gus."

Rusty walked back down to the cabin and started making plans on how to fix the cabin up so he could spend some weekends there. Rusty spent the rest of the afternoon there and decided it was time to go back to the valley. When he started walking to his truck, he had a strange feeling that someone was watching him. He turned and looked around and didn't see anyone or anything that could make him feel that way. He thought to himself, *Maybe they are the spirits here after all.* He got in his truck and left and went back to his home. All of the following week, Rusty had that Indian burial ground on his mind. He told Sally about what he was going to do that following weekend, and he wanted her to start getting some information on what he could do about making the place look better. Sally started looking at pictures that she thought would make the burial site look better. After she gathered all the materials she had looked at, she gave it to Rusty and told him, "Some of these pictures might be what you're interested in."

Rusty took the information and put it in his office and thought about what he was going to do.

The weekend finally came, and Saturday morning, Rusty loaded up some tools and headed up for the mountains. When he got there at the burial site, Gus was standing there, waiting on him. Rusty and Gus got the tools out of the truck and started cleaning the grave sites. They worked all day Saturday and got the grave sites looking much better. They restocked the rocks on the graves and made them look better. They finished up the work, and Rusty offered to pay Gus for his help. Gus refused to take any money and told Rusty he was glad to be able to help. He just started walking away, and Rusty asked him if he could drive him up to where he was living.

"No, I enjoy walking, and I don't have too far to go."

Rusty got back in his truck and drove down to the cabin. He kept having this strange feeling and decided to walk around and look to see if he could figure out what it was. After walking around and looking, he still couldn't come up with any reason why he felt that way. Rusty walked back to the cabin, looked inside, came back out, got in his truck, and headed back to the valley. Rusty got back to the office on Monday morning. He discussed all the work they were going to be doing for the upcoming week. Rusty told Mark he was making him a superintendent over all the jobs he had going. "You will be in charge, and you will let me know at the end of the day how each job is going."

After the Monday morning meeting was over, Sally told Rusty the mayor of Indian Springs had called and wanted to meet with him at his office. "He wants you to meet him there around ten o'clock this morning, if you can make it."

"Call him and tell him I'll be there at ten o'clock."

Rusty met with the mayor at ten o'clock, and they discussed several things that the city was trying to do to accommodate all the new people moving into Indian Springs. "We are going to need a lot more houses built, and we thought maybe you might be interested in building some of those houses!"

"Well, Mayor, I have been thinking about that for a while now. I've decided to build a model home on the northeast corner of my property. I plan to start clearing some land next month to start my project."

"Well, that's great news, Rusty, and I'm sure you will be building nice houses. You have a good reputation for doing quality work, and I'm sure you will do well in the house-building business."

"Mayor, I appreciate you, and I will let you know how things are going in the future."

Rusty left the mayor's office and went back to his office. He gave Sally a list of names he wanted her to call and make appointments with. All the people that were on the list met with Rusty, and he told them the plans he had for building the houses. He met with the contractors to clear the land of all the timber. Rusty got with all the engineers designing the roads and lots for the houses. He got with the excavating contractor and lined them up on the building of the roads. His plan was to build six hundred new homes on the property. The timber cutters came in and started cutting the trees, and the surveyors came in behind them and started laying out the streets and lots for the houses. When the news got out about Rusty's big subdivision being built, a lot of other people and businesses started moving into the valley. With all the new construction, there would be a lot of people moving in the valley and looking for new jobs and new opportunities. Rusty knew, with all this new building going on, he was going to have to hire a lot more people and create more jobs for the people in the valley. There would be new schools and more public facilities being built. This would create jobs for his company to get bigger and bigger. Rusty went by his office on Saturday morning, and Sally was sitting at her desk.

"What are you doing here on Saturday, Sally?"

"I guess I'm going to have to start working every Saturday, Rusty. I have so much work to do. I can't get it all done in one week."

"Well, you need to hire a new helper, Sally."

I've also been thinking about that, Rusty. I have a friend whose daughter just graduated from high school and needs a job. I thought I would call her and see if she would be interested in coming to work here."

"That will be fine with me, Sally. Go ahead and get you some help."

"What are you doing here today, Rusty?"

"Well, the city is planning on building a new school, and they will be taking bids next week, and I'm planning on bidding on the project. They are sending me the drawings, and I want to be ready to bid on them as soon as I get the drawings. I'm going to be getting prices on materials today."

Sally and Rusty worked all day that Saturday. And when they got ready to leave that afternoon, Rusty told Sally, "I'm going to give you a big raise for all the hard work you do, Sally."

"You don't have to do that, Rusty, but I do appreciate it."

Monday morning came, and after the regular Monday meeting, Rusty asked Mark to come into his office. Mark walked into his office and sat down and said, "What's up, boss?"

"Mark, you know our office is getting a little crowded. Sally has hired a new helper, and we need new office space. This is what

I have been thinking about for a couple of weeks. I have some plans here for a new office building. We have outgrown this old building. I want you to put Jesse in charge of all the small projects tomorrow morning. Mark, you will be in charge of building a new office building. We're going to build it behind the old building here, and I want you to start breaking ground tomorrow. It's going to be a large three-story building and should take care of all the needs that we will have in the near future. When the new building is complete, I want you to remove this old building and increase the size of the parking lot. I would like some new trees planted around the parking lots and lots of new plants."

As time passed by, Rusty got his model homes built and started building new houses. The new office building was almost complete and was a real showplace for the community. The old building was gone now, and the parking lot was enlarged. Mark did a great job with the landscaping. Mark told Rusty the bottom floor of the new office building was ready to be moved into, and the second and third floors would be finished within the month.

"That's great news, Mark. We will start moving in tomorrow."

Sally and her helper each had their own office. There were five more offices on the first floor for future employees. Rusty's office was on the main floor in the back of the building. The conference room for the company would be on the second floor, and all the blueprints and design materials would be on the third floor. Rusty's marquee and sign for Wilson Construction Company was on the face of the third floor of the building. Rusty, Mark, Jesse, and Sally stood out front of the building, looking at how nice the building was, and Rusty said, "I wish my grandpa could see this now."

Sally said, "Well, maybe he can, Rusty."

Chapter 6

Wilson Construction Company was now one of the biggest contractors in the state of Tennessee. They were beginning to get calls from all over the Southeast to build office buildings for different companies. Rusty was continuing to hire new employees; he now had over seventeen superintendents, running jobs for him and different parts of the state. A new company had moved into Indian Springs. They purchased sixty acres of farmland and had plans to build a new mini mall. With Rusty's new subdivision, they were now building and completing one house every three weeks. These houses were selling as fast as they built them. Rusty bought a four-acre tract of land next to the main office. He decided to build an apartment building because some of the employees wanted to rent an apartment, and there were none to be had, so Rusty decided to build one. It didn't take long for him to get this apartment building built, and now it was ready to be occupied. One day, a man walked into the office building and asked the receptionist if the company was hiring anybody. She said, "Yes. Would you like to fill out an application?"

"Yes, I would."

"What is your name, sir?"

"My name is Bob Ford."

The receptionist told him to go over and sit down, and she would have someone come and get him. She called Sally and told her there was a Mr. Ford in the lobby and was looking for a job. Sally told the receptionist she would be out in just a minute to get him. Bob sat there for about five minutes, and then Sally came out and said, "Will you come with me, sir?" Sally walked into a room and gave him an application to fill out. "I'll be back in here to get it. Take your time. There's no rush."

Bob finished filling out the application and sat there and waited on Sally to come back and get it. Sally finally walked in and asked Bob if he was finished. Bob said yes.

Sally told Bob, "I will turn your application in and will be back to get you in just a few minutes. Rusty, Mark, and Jesse were sitting in the conference room, talking about a contract they were going to get with a large corporation. Sally walked into the conference room and told Rusty she had an application for a man, and he was waiting next to her office. She handed Rusty the application, and he and Mark went over it. Sally stood there while they were studying the application, and Rusty told her, "Bring him in here, and we'll talk to him." Sally left and went and got Bob and brought him to the conference room. Sally introduced Bob to everybody, and Rusty asked him to have a seat. Rusty said, "I see where you are from: Alabama."

"I moved up here and bought a little small farmhouse just outside the city limits. I've been working here for about four months. I have a job with a service station, but it does not pay very much. I thought I might find a construction job and maybe make a little more money."

"Have you ever done construction work, Bob?"

"Yes, I did some work in construction for my uncle."

"Well, we can always use more help, Bob. When would you like to start?"

"I would like to start as soon as I can."

Jesse spoke up and said, "So your name is Bob Ford?"

"Yes, it is."

"Are you any kin to the Bob Ford that killed Jesse James?"

Bob said, "I don't think so."

Jesse started laughing. Rusty spoke up and said, "Don't pay any attention to him, Bob. He's just trying to be funny."

Rusty hired Bob that day, but little did he know that hiring Bob would change his life forever. Several months had passed, and it was springtime in the mountains again. Rusty went to work on Friday morning and told Sally he was going up to the cabin and spending the weekend. "If anybody needs me, they can call me." Rusty left Saturday morning going up to the cabin. When he got to the cabin, Gus was standing at his front door.

"Hello, Gus. What are you doing here?"

"Well, Rusty, I had a feeling you were coming up today, so I decided to stand down here and wait till you got here."

"Well, here I am, Gus. What's going on?"

"Two days ago, Rusty, I came by the burial ground, and there were some teenagers throwing the rocks on the graves over the side. I have been placing them back for the last two days. I ran them off, but we need to do something to keep the people out of there."

"Well, Gus, let's walk up there and have a look."

Rusty and Gus walked up to the burial grounds and looked around and decided what they were going to do. Rusty said, "This is what I'm going to do Monday: I'm going to get a fence contractor to come up here and put a fence around the burial site. We'll make it tall enough that no one can climb over it. We'll put a nice gate on it and make sure it can be locked up."

"That sounds good, Rusty. That will make the spirits very happy."

"I don't know about the spirits, Gus, but maybe it'll make you happy, and that's all that matters."

They stood around and talked for a while, and Gus left, and Rusty walked back down to the cabin. Rusty spent the rest of the weekend fixing stuff inside the cabin to make it look a little better. He left Sunday afternoon and went back to the valley. Monday rolled around, and Rusty was on the phone, looking for a fence contractor to go up to the cabin. A few days later, a fence contractor came by with some pictures to show Rusty. The fence would be twelve feet tall and had these fancy little ornaments in between the rails. The gate would be four feet wide with a lock on it; they would put an arch over the gate that would read "Native American." Rusty liked everything the contractor showed him and asked him when he could go up and build the fence. Rusty said, "Meet me early tomorrow morning, and I will take you up there and show you where to build the fence."

Rusty left the next morning with a contractor and went up to the cabin. They walked up to where the burial site was. The contractor looked around and said, "I will have a crew up here tomorrow morning, putting a fence up, if that's what you want."

"How long will it take you to do this?" Rusty asked.

"It'll take about three days," the contractor said, "and will call you when it's completed."

Rusty thanked the man and told him to get started. Three days passed, and the contractor called Rusty and said, "The job is finished."

Rusty drove up there that day and looked at it, and he was amazed how good it looked. He stood there looking at the site and said, "All we need now is a marble bench inside the fence to sit on when you want to visit with the spirits. I know Gus will really like this."

That weekend, Rusty drove back up to the cabin and decided to spend the whole weekend, doing nothing.

He sat on the front porch in a rocking chair that he had purchased the week before. He saw a deer running across the front yard and down the mountainside. He thought to himself, *I think it was my destiny to own this cabin. This is my most favorite place in the world.* Rusty was thirty-one years old now and his construction company, and the cabin was the only thing in his life that seemed to be important. He kept thinking, *There has to be something else. But what is it?* He just didn't know. As destiny would have it, something big was fixing to change his life.

Chapter 7

One afternoon, Bob walked into Rusty's office and asked Rusty if he would ride up to his house on Saturday. "I want to do some remodeling, and I was wondering if you would help me out on it. If you would come up and look at my house and show me what I need to do. I will have my wife to fix dinner."

Rusty agreed to go to Bob's house and see what he needed to do. When Rusty got there, Bob took him into the foyer and said, "I want to build a stairwell up to the attic. I want to build a bonus room for when I have company."

Rusty told him, "That would be an easy and simple job to do."

Bob asked, "Do you think I could use some of the men on the job to help me do this, Rusty?"

"Yes, Bob, I will get you a list of materials that you are going to need. You buy the material, and I'll furnish the labor to do the work. The labor won't cost you anything. I'll get Mark and Jesse and two or three of the other men to come up and help. We can probably do what you need to do in one day. We will come up on a Saturday, and maybe your wife can cook dinner for everybody."

"I'll make sure she does that, Rusty. I'll let you know as soon as I get the material, and we can do it one Saturday."

Kathy walked out into the hallway, where Bob and Rusty were standing. Bob said, "Oh, by the way, Rusty, this is my wife, Kathy."

Rusty said, "I am pleased to meet you, Ms. Ford. We will be glad to come up here and help Bob do his work in the hallway here."

Kathy said thank you and turned and walked back into the kitchen. Two weeks passed, and Bob told Rusty he had all the materials ready to do the remodeling.

"Okay, Bob, I'll get the men ready next Saturday, and we'll come up and do the work."

Rusty and the crew arrived the next Saturday morning at Bob's house. They got all their tools out and went in the house and started to work. While they were working that morning, Bob's wife was preparing lunch for them all. At twelve o'clock that day, they all sat down and had dinner. Everyone complimented Ms. Ford for the fine dinner. After dinner, they all went back to work. Rusty and Kathy were standing around, talking to each other while their work was going on. The work was almost completed when Bob walked up and told Kathy, "Why are you standing here talking? You need to go and clean the kitchen up."

"Okay, I will, Bob."

Kathy turned and walked into the kitchen. They finished up the work and were loading up all their tools. Bob walked out on the porch and thanked everyone for coming up and helping him work on his house. Kathy walked to the front door and waved goodbye to everybody.

Rusty told Bob, "We'll see you Monday at work."

Rusty and Mark got in the truck and started down the road, and Mark said, "He sure is mean to his wife, isn't he?"

"Yes, it seems like he is. She's a very beautiful woman, isn't she, Rusty?"

"Yes, I will definitely have to agree with you on that."

After everybody left, Bob told Kathy, "You sure was hanging around my boss an awful lot today."

Kathy replied, "I was just trying to be nice to the man that was working for you free of charge."

"Well, I don't want you to be nice to anyone, Kathy. They may get the wrong idea."

Monday morning came, and everybody was back at work on their jobs. About noontime, Rusty told Sally, "I'm going to ride downtown to the supermarket. I'll be back in a little while."

Rusty was walking through the supermarket, picking up a few things, when he ran into Kathy.

"Hello, Ms. Ford. Nice seeing you again."

Kathy wouldn't look at Rusty but said hello.

Rusty turned his head to look sideways and said, "I noticed a big bruise on the side of your face. What happened to your face, Kathy? It looks like you have a big bruise there."

"Bob hit me because I spent too much time with you while they were doing the work on the house."

"I'm sorry, Kathy, about this. I will say something to him if you want me to."

"No, Rusty. If you say anything, it will just make things worse." Then Kathy turned and walked away.

Rusty went back to the office and sat down at his desk and was wondering why Bob was so mean to his wife. The next day, Rusty told Mark about what happened, and Mark said, "It's best to stay out of their personal problems, Rusty."

Rusty said, "She's a beautiful person and does not deserve to be treated like that. No woman does."

A few days passed, and Rusty could not get it off his mind that a man who worked for him would abuse his wife like that. The next day, after work, Jesse came by the office and told Mark he needed to talk to Rusty about Bob.

"Well, he's in his office. Go in there and talk to him."

Jesse walked into Rusty's office and said, "I need to talk to you about Bob."

"All right, Jesse, what's going on?"

"Well, I said something to Bob about how everybody enjoyed the dinner she made for us that day we worked for them, and he got mad and said everybody needs to stay away from her. So what do you think's going on, Rusty?"

"I don't know, Jesse, but don't worry about it. I'll have a talk with Bob first chance I get."

A few days went by, and Bob seemed to be doing better on the job, so Rusty decided not to say anything to him at this time. Sally walked into Rusty's office and said, "We got a phone call from a company in Little Rock, Arkansas. They want you to give them a price on building a new office facility for them. Here's their number. You can call them when you're ready."

Rusty's company was now doing work all over Tennessee. "We may start doing work all over the southeast."

Rusty called and set up an appointment with a company in Arkansas and agreed to fly out there the next day. Rusty got with Mark, and the next day, they flew to Little Rock. The coal mine and company wanted a ten-story office building built in Little Rock. The company office manager told Rusty he had heard a lot about Wilson Construction and how good their company was.

"We would like you to take our drawings and give us a price on building this office building for us." They took Rusty and Mark to the site where they wanted the building to be built. The engineers had already got the property approved for the building. Rusty told the company manager he would take the drawings back to his office and would get back in touch in about three days. Mark and Rusty flew back to Indian Springs and began working on the drawings. They spent the next two days getting the prices on everything and had a price ready to give to the coal company. The next day, Rusty and Mark flew back out to Arkansas, met with a coal company, and the managers gave them a price on what the building was going to cost. Nicole's company managers agreed with the price and signed the contract with Wilson Construction Company to do the work. Rusty agreed to start the job the following week. They flew back to Indian Springs and started getting everything ready to send a crew to Arkansas to do the job. Rusty told Mark he was going to be the one in charge of the building of the office building.

"Choose the men you want to take out there with you."

Mark gathered all the crews working for Wilson Construction and told them about the Arkansas job. "We're going to need six men to go to Arkansas. Those that want to go will be paid extra money for their work. The company will pay all expenses while they're there. You will have to go and stay two weeks at a time. The company will furnish you transportation back and forth from Indian Springs to Little Rock on the weekends that you come home."

Bob and five men volunteered to go. Mark had all the men he was planning on taking and told them to be ready to go on Monday. Bob went home that afternoon and told Kathy he would be working out of town. "I will be working for two weeks and come home for the weekend. I don't want you going anywhere or doing anything without me knowing about it!"

Kathy said, "I'm not your slave, Bob, and I didn't move in with you to be treated like one."

"You just do what I tell you, Kathy, and we'll get along just fine!"

Sunday afternoon, before Bob was supposed to leave on Monday, he went to his next-door neighbor's house. He told his neighbor he would be working out of town and would like for him to keep an eye on his house and what goes on there!

The neighbor agreed to watch out for his place. Bob left Monday morning with the rest of the crew and headed for Little Rock. A few days passed, and Sally said she needed something from the hardware store, so Rusty agreed to go downtown and get whatever she needed. While he was there in the store, he saw a taxi pull up in front, and Kathy got out of it. She walked into the hardware store, and Rusty said, "Hello, Kathy. How are you doing?"

Kathy said, "I'm doing fine."

"How are you? What are you doing getting out of a taxi? Is there something wrong with your car?"

"No, Rusty, there's nothing wrong with my car."

Bob took the keys with him, and he told me not to be driving it while he was gone out of town working. I needed a few things for the house, and I decided to come down and get them."

"Well, when you're finished shopping, would you like for me to drive you back home?"

"Yes, that would be nice, Rusty. I would appreciate it very much."

Rusty finished shopping for the things that he needed and waited for Kathy to finish. She finally walked up to Rusty and said, "Okay, I'm ready to go now, Rusty."

They got in Rusty's truck and headed back to Bob's house. On the way there, Rusty asked Kathy if she was having any problems with Bob. "Is there anything I can help you with?"

"There's a lot I would like to tell you about, but now is not the time."

"Well, whenever you get ready to talk to me, Kathy, I will be glad to come by and get you, and we'll go somewhere and just sit down and talk for a while."

"That would be nice, Rusty. I will give you a call."

Rusty dropped Kathy off at her house that day and didn't hear from her anymore for a couple of weeks. Two weeks had passed. Bob came home for the weekend and asked the neighbor if anything went on while he was gone. The neighbors saw Kathy leave in a taxi and saw when Rusty dropped her off. He didn't tell Bob any of that because he was afraid Bob would harm Kathy. Bob continued to go to Arkansas and come back on the weekends. Three months had passed, and Rusty has never heard anything from Kathy. Then one day, the phone rang, and it was Kathy.

"Hello, Rusty, how are you?"

"I'm doing fine, Kathy. How are you?"

"I was wondering if you could meet me somewhere tomorrow? I would love to talk to you."

"Yes, Kathy, I would be glad to meet you wherever you would like."

"Can you meet me at the park tomorrow at noontime?"

"Yes, I would be glad to meet you there, Kathy."

"Okay, Rusty, I'll see you then."

The next day, at noontime, Rusty drove to the park, and Kathy was sitting at one of the tables.

"Hello, Kathy. It's nice to see you again. How have you been doing?"

"I'm doing okay, Rusty. There's a lot I want to talk to you about."

"Okay, Kathy, tell me all about it."

"Bob and I are not married. We have been divorced for several years now."

"Well, why are you still with him, Kathy?"

"It's a long story. Do you want to hear about it?"

"Yes, I would like to hear, and maybe I can help you."

"Okay, I was only seventeen years old when I met Bob. My sister's husband introduced me to him. At that time, he seemed like a real nice and very polite person. We went to movies together, and he always treated me real nice. We dated for several months, and my father kept telling me to stay away from him. He didn't like Bob. He said there was something about him that he just didn't like. Well, I didn't listen, and I kept dating Bob. He told me he loves me, and he wanted to get married. So we got married. I didn't realize what a mistake I had made until later on. He began to be a little abusive, and I thought it might just be because of the job he had. He didn't make very much money, and things were very hard to start out with. We moved into a little garage apartment in a small town right outside of Birmingham. We were both born and grew up in Birmingham. We had been living in the garage apartment for about four months when I found out I was pregnant. I waited a couple of months before I told Bob, and he got really angry with me. He asked me why I did that. 'You know we can't afford to have a baby right now.' I told Bob I thought he wanted children, and he said, 'Not right now.' The next day, I went over to my sister's house to fix her hair. She was going to a party that night and wanted to look real good. So I spent all afternoon rolling her hair and getting her ready to go to her party. When I got home that afternoon, Bob was already home from work. He was standing at the top of the stairs on a little balcony that goes into the apartment. As I was walking up the steps, he was asking me where I had been, and I told him that I had been rolling my sister's hair.

"When I reached the top of the stairs, he grabbed me and told me I was not supposed to go anywhere without him knowing about it. He was shaking me and shoved me backward, and I fell down the stairs. The next thing I remember, I've been lying in the hospital for four days. I was almost six months pregnant at the time, and the doctors told me that the baby had died in the fall. I had three broken ribs, and one of my legs was broken in three places. I went into shock after I heard about the baby and had to have a lot of counseling. The police questioned Bob about the incident, and he told them that I had tripped and fell down the stairs. I told the police that he had pushed me down the stairs. They said there was nothing they could do without a witness. It was my word against his. I was in the hospital for several weeks, and after I got out, I filed for a divorce and moved back in with my father.

"My mother had died when I was just a small girl and my father was a coal miner. He got injured in the mines and wasn't able to walk. I never did get a job. I just took care of my father. My sister and her husband were living with my father when I moved back in. They moved across the street to a little apartment. and I stayed there with my father. My father kept telling me, 'I told you that man was no good before you married him.' He told me when he died, he was leaving the house to my sister because he didn't want Bob winding up with anything he had. I took care of my father for several years, and when he died, he left the house to my sister. They moved in, and I stayed with them. One day I got a phone call from Bob, asking me to move to Tennessee. He said he had bought a house, and he was going to fix it up real good, and he wanted me to come back and live with him. He promised to make up for all the bad times that he had been mean to me. He said that he had changed, and he would be good to me. He kept calling every night for two weeks, begging me to come back to Tennessee and live with him. My sister told me they wanted the house by themselves, and I should move back in with Bob. The next time Bob called, I told him that I would move back in with him. I told him to come to Alabama and get me. The next day, Bob showed up in a brand-new pickup truck and told me he had a good job with a construction company.

"My sister kept insisting on me living with Bob, so I packed up my clothes and loaded up and went with him. Now here I am with him again, and he's the same old Bob. He treats me very badly, and I want to leave, but I have no place to go."

"You're a beautiful woman, Kathy. You look like a princess, and you deserve a better life than what you're living. If you want to leave Bob, I will let you move into one of my apartments. You can find a job here in town, and you can make a better life for yourself."

"Mr. Smith down at the hardware store is looking for a cashier, and I'm sure you can get a job there. Go down and talk to him. And if he puts you to work, I'll help you move all your things into one of my apartments."

"I appreciate you helping me Rusty, but I'm afraid what Bob might do when he finds out I have left him."

"Don't worry about Bob, princess. There's plenty of people around that will protect you."

Rusty and Kathy left the park and went down to the hardware store. Kathy walked in and talked to Mr. Smith about a job.

"Well, Kathy, I need a cashier. And if Rusty's recommended you, I'll put you to work. When would you like to start?"

"As soon as I could, Mr. Smith."

"Will you come in tomorrow morning at eight o'clock, and you can start to work?"

"Thank you, Mr. Smith. I will be here."

Rusty and Kathy left. They arrived at Bob's house, and Kathy went in and started bringing all her belongings out to Rusty's truck. They put everything Kathy had and drove down to the apartment building. Rusty called Sally at the office and told her to bring down a lease and a key to one of the apartments. They waited until Sally arrived with a key and then began moving Kathy's things into the apartment. Kathy signed the lease agreement, and Rusty called and had the water and power turned on. Sally left and went back to the office.

"If you need transportation, princess, I have an extra car at the office you can use if you need it."

"Thank you, Rusty, but I can walk to work tomorrow. It's only a few blocks from here."

"Well, if you need anything, just let me know."

"Okay. Thanks, Rusty. I'll see you later."

Rusty left and went back to the office, walked back into the office, and sat down. Sally walked into Rusty's office and said, "What's going on, Rusty, with Bob's wife?"

"She's not his wife."

"Well, he's been telling everybody she was his wife."

"I know that's what he's been saying. It's a long story, and I will let her tell you if she wants you to know."

The next day, Rusty went down to the police headquarters and went in and talked to his friend Paul. He told Paul what was going on with Bob and his ex-wife, Kathy. He told Paul that he had moved her into an apartment and would like for someone to watch out for her on the weekends.

Paul told Rusty, "I will be glad to have someone watch that area all weekend."

"Well, I'm not sure how Bob is going to handle this, but I think he will be very upset about it."

"Don't worry about it, Rusty. We'll keep an eye on things out there."

"Thank you, sir. I appreciate it very much."

Rusty left for his office and felt a little more secure that Kathy would be okay.

Chapter 8

That weekend, Jesse and his crew returned to Indian Springs. When Bob got home, he saw that Kathy had left with all of her belongings. He walked over to his next-door neighbor and asked him if he had seen Kathy. He said, "Yes, I saw her and a man in a new white Ford pickup load all her things up and left."

"Do you know who the man was?"

"Yes, it was Rusty Wilson, the man you work for."

Bob jumped in his truck and headed down to Rusty's office. When he got there, he walked in, and the only person in the office was Rusty. Rusty walked out of his office and met Bob in the lobby.

"Good to see you again, Bob. What's going on?"

"Well, that's what I was going to ask you, Rusty! When I got home, I found out that Kathy had moved out, and I was wondering where she was. She is in one of my apartments down the street!"

"She asked me if I would help her move from your house to the apartment, and I agreed to help her."

"Do you know why she moved out, Rusty?"

"Well, she told me that you and her were having problems, and she didn't want to stay there anymore so I helped her move."

"What kind of problems did she say we were having?"

"She said you were very abusive to her, and she didn't want to live there anymore. Let me say this, Bob, I don't want to get into your personal problem, but I told her I would try to help anyway I could."

"Rusty!"

"I'm not getting involved with her, Bob. She asked for my help, and that's what I was going to do to help her. I think you should call her and discuss this with her!"

"I don't want to call her, Rusty. I want to go see her. Can you tell me where she's at?"

"I will tell you what apartment she's living in, but first I want to call her and tell her you're on your way over there. Bob, I want you to know that property belongs to me, and I don't want you to cause any trouble there! She's in apartment 4."

Bob turned and walked out, got in his truck, and headed over to the apartments. Rusty called Kathy and told her Bob was on his way over. He also called the police department and told them what was going on and to make sure there was no trouble. They told Rusty there was a police officer already there, and he would make sure nothing was going to happen.

When Bob arrived at the apartment, Kathy was standing on the balcony outside her door. Bob walked up the steps and asked Kathy what was she doing there.

"I've moved out on my own, Bob! I have a job now, and I'm going to take care of myself."

"You belong to me, Kathy, and you're going back to my house!"

"I'm not going anywhere with you, Bob."

At that moment, the police officer stepped out of his car and was standing, looking up at Kathy and Bob. He asked Kathy if she was having any problem, and Kathy answered, "No, he's leaving right now." She looked at Bob and said, "You better leave now, Bob!"

"I'll see you later, Kathy." Bob turned and started walking down the steps and stopped and looked back up at Kathy and said, "This is not over yet."

Kathy turned and went back into her apartment and closed the door. Bob got in his truck and drove away.

Kathy called Rusty and told him Bob had just left. "He was very angry, and I'm afraid he might come back."

"Just stay in your apartment, princess, and don't worry. The police officer will be there all weekend!"

The weekend passed, and the crew gathered Monday morning, ready to go back to Arkansas. Bob never showed up. Jesse called Bob and asked him where he was, and they were getting ready to leave. Bob told Jesse, "I'm not going back to Arkansas."

"What are you going to do, Bob? Are you quitting the company?"

"No, I'm not quitting the company. I want to work with another crew here in town."

"Well, you'll have to talk to Rusty about that, Bob."

Jesse told Rusty what Bob had said about working with another crew.

"Well, Jesse, I'll have to see what we can do about that."

Bob never showed up at the office that day. He went all over town, wondering how he was going to get Kathy back. He went to every place in town, looking to see if he could find where Kathy was working. He found her at the hardware store and asked her once again if she was moving back into his house. She said, "No, I'm staying right where I am."

"Well, you still belong to me, Kathy."

"I don't belong to anybody, Bob. I am my own person now, and I don't want you bothering me!"

Bob left the hardware store and told Kathy he would see her later. Rusty tried calling Bob for the next two days to find out if he was planning on coming back to work. Bob never answered his phone. Rusty finally drove out to Bob's house to talk to him. Bob was standing outside, putting something in his truck, when Rusty drove up. Rusty got out of his truck and walked up to Bob and said, "I tried to get in touch with you to find out if you were coming back to work."

"No, Rusty, I'm not coming back to work for you. I'm thinking about selling my house and moving back to Alabama."

"Well, if there's any way I can help you, Bob, let me know."

Rusty got back in his truck and drove back to the office. Rusty told Sally, "Find out how much we owed Bob and send him some money. He no longer works for us." Several nights passed, and Bob could be seen sitting in the parking lot at the apartment where Kathy was living. Finally, the police drove up to where Bob was parked and asked him what he was doing in the parking lot.

"I was sitting here waiting to visit a friend of mine."

"Who is your friend?" the police officer asked.

"Her name is Kathy, and she lives in the apartment."

"I know Kathy. She's at home right now. Do you want me to go get her for you?"

"No, that's okay, I'm going to leave now."

Bob drove out of the parking lot and went back to his house. The next day, Bob loaded all his belongings in his truck and drove down to the office to see Rusty.

"I would like to talk to Rusty if he's in."

"He's in his office, Bob. I'll tell him you're coming in to see him."

She buzzed Rusty and said, "Bob's here to see you."

"Send him in."

Sally said, "You can go in now, Bob."

Bob walked into Rusty's office and told Rusty, "I've got all my things loaded in my truck, and I'm headed back to Alabama. I know you had something to do with Kathy moving out of my house."

"Bob, I had nothing to do with her leaving you. You brought all this on yourself by the way you treated her. So you can't blame anybody but yourself."

"Well, I blame you, Rusty, and I hope you're satisfied."

"The only thing I've done, Bob, is I thought I was helping someone who needed help."

"So long, Rusty. Maybe I'll come back this way someday. And if I do, I'll pay you a visit!"

"Well, keep in touch, Bob."

Bob left the office and got in his truck and drove away. Several months had passed since Bob left Indian Springs. Rusty and Kathy started spending a lot of time together; they were seen together all over town. People were wondering if maybe they were having an affair together. They were seen at all the major events in Indian Springs. One Saturday afternoon, Rusty and Kathy were at the park, and Kathy said to Rusty, "I'm falling in love with you, Rusty."

"I'm glad to hear that, princess, because I feel the same way about you."

Several people asked Kathy if she and Rusty were planning to get married. She replied, "I don't know. He hasn't asked me yet."

As time passed, Rusty's business was getting bigger and bigger, and he had to do a lot of traveling. He and Kathy continued to see each other. One weekend, Rusty asked Kathy if she would ride up into the mountains where the cabin was. She said, "Yes, I've heard a lot about this cabin, and I would like to see it!"

They drove up there that weekend, and Kathy said she loved the cabin.

Rusty told her, "If we ever get married, this is where I would like to spend our honeymoon."

"Well, we're not going to get married unless you ask me, Rusty."

"Well, I'm asking you, will you marry me, princess?"

"Yes, I will, Rusty. I was wondering when you were going to ask me."

"Well, I've been thinking about it for a while now."

They spent the rest of the day at the cabin and were getting ready to leave. They were standing by Rusty's truck, and Kathy said, "It feels like someone's watching us!"

"I know, princess. I have that feeling every time I come up here. A friend of mine named Gus says it's nothing to worry about. It's only the spirits. It's all good spirits."

"Well, I'm not afraid, Rusty, as long as you're with me."

"Don't worry, princess. I will always take care of you."

They left that afternoon and headed back down to Indian Springs. The next day, Rusty had a meeting with Sally and Mark and told them that he had asked Kathy to marry him. "She said yes, but we haven't set a date yet. But we're hoping within the next month or two. What I need you to do, Mark, is the company is getting so big now. We need to hire more people. We need to get more men for crew leaders. We need superintendents for the jobs that we're going to be doing in Kentucky, Tennessee, North Carolina, South Carolina, Arkansas, and Georgia. I'll be flying all over the Southeast and getting bids on these jobs, and I need a man to take them over once we get the contract signed."

"Okay, Rusty, I'll start looking for a new man tomorrow."

The next day, Mark ran ads and all the newspapers, asking for people to apply for the new job coming up. Men all over the Southeast began answering the ads for the job. Early one Saturday morning, Rusty got a call from Gus up on Dogwood Mountain.

"Hello, Gus, how are you doing?"

"I'm doing fine, Rusty. I wanted to let you know I was walking down the road about a mile past the cabin when I saw a man in a red pickup stopped, and he asked me if you were at the cabin. I told him I didn't think so, and he told me he was a friend of yours. I asked him what his name was, and he said he was just a friend of yours, and you told him it was okay for him to hunt deer by your cabin. Then he drove up to your cabin. I noticed he had an Alabama license plate on the back of his truck when he drove away.

"Well, Gus, I haven't told anybody they could hunt on the property. I'll come up there this morning and check it out. Thanks for letting me know, Gus, and I'll talk to you later."

"Okay, Rusty. Be careful."

That morning, Rusty left to go up to the cabin on the mountain. When he arrived at the cabin, there was no one around. He could see tire tracks where somebody had been driving in and out of the road going to the cabin. From the description of the truck, it sounded like it might be Bob's. What Bob was doing up here at my cabin seemed awfully strange. Rusty decided to call Mark and let him know what was going on and tell him where he was at. Mark said, "Be careful, Rusty. If it's Bob, he may start some trouble with you."

"I'll be all right, Mark. I'll be back in town before dark."

It started getting late, and Rusty decided to walk down to the edge of the mountain and look down where the deer would come down and drink water on the ledge down below. While Rusty was standing there, he heard a noise behind him. He turned and looked around, and it was a red pickup coming down the driveway. The man got out of the pickup and walked down and said, "Hello, Rusty, nice to see you again."

It was Bob, and he had a gun in his hand."

"What are you doing here, Bob? I thought you went back to Alabama?"

"I did go back to Alabama, Rusty, but I thought I would come up here and thank you for taking my woman away from me."

"She's not your woman anymore, Bob, and you're just going to have to live with that."

"Well, Rusty, I was thinking, the only way I will ever get her back is to get rid of you."

"What are you planning on doing, Bob, shoot me? You know you'll never get away with this, Bob."

Bob pointed the gun at Rusty and fired. The bullet struck Rusty in the middle of his chest and his body fell over the edge of the mountain, down about 190 feet. His body landed on the pile of rocks next to the pool of water, where the deer would come down and the water in the afternoons. Bob walked over to the edge of the mountain and looked down and saw Rusty's body lying there.

Bob said, "Well, Rusty, I guess I'll get back with her now that you're out of the picture." Bob turned and walked up to his truck and started driving away. He thought he saw someone standing at the gate at the burial ground, but when he got there, no one was there.

He heard a strange noise coming from the burial ground, but no one was there. He didn't see anyone, so he headed down the mountain to go back to Indian Springs. When he got to Indian Springs, he parked his truck in the parking lot across the street from Kathy's apartment. He sat there for a while, thinking what he was going to do next. Bob decided to go up and knock on Kathy's door and ask her one more time to go back to Alabama with him. When he knocked on the door, Kathy opened and saw Bob standing there.

"What are you doing here, Bob? I thought you were in Alabama?"

"I was in Alabama, Kathy. I came back to see if you wanted to move back with me?"

"No, Bob, I'm not going anywhere with you. I told you I have nothing to do with you anymore."

"Well, I heard you and Rusty were planning to get married, but I don't think you'll have to worry about that anymore."

What do you mean, Bob?"

"Well, let's just say things have changed around here a little bit. And if you decide you want to come back to Alabama with me, I'll be waiting for you."

Kathy called Sally and told her Bob had just left and was acting very strange. "I tried calling Rusty, and I couldn't get any answer from him. I don't know what's going on. I'm very scared. Don't worry, Kathy, I'll try to get in touch with Rusty, and I'll let him know what's happening."

Sally called and tried to get in touch with Rusty, but there was no answer, so she called Mark. "Mark, I've been trying to get in touch with Rusty, and there's no answer on his phone. Bob just left the apartment where Kathy lives, and she's very worried about Rusty."

"I'll try to get in touch with Rusty, and I'll let you know what I find out." Mark tried calling Rusty several times during the night and could never get in touch with him. Mark began to worry. He thought something might have happened to Rusty.

Chapter 9

Mark was thinking maybe Rusty just decided to spend the night at the cabin and had misplaced his phone. He told Sally he would drive up in the morning if he didn't get any answers from Rusty. The next morning, no one had heard from Rusty, so Mark decided to drive up to the cabin to see what was going on. When he got to the cabin that morning, Rusty's truck was sitting there, but Rusty was nowhere to be found. He was not in the cabin, so Mark walked up to the Indian burial site. He looked all around the burial site, and there was no sign of Rusty. Mark started walking back down the hill to the cabin when he saw Gus walk up.

"Hello. Are you Looking for Rusty?"

"Yes, I am. Who are you?"

"My name is Gus. I'm a friend of Rusty's."

"We've been trying to get in touch with Rusty all night, and I decided to come up today to find him. His truck is here, but he is nowhere to be found. Have you seen him?"

"No, I haven't seen him, but I heard a gunshot late yesterday afternoon. I saw a red truck leaving the cabin and headed down the mountain. I walked down to the cabin to see if Rusty was there, and I never could find him."

"Well, I guess I'm going to call the county sheriff and have them come up here."

"Well, I'll help you look for him when they get here."

About an hour later, the county sheriffs arrived and began to investigate the area. They told Mark they were going to arrange for a search party to start looking all over the mountain for Rusty. The state troopers and the FBI were called in to help the search for Rusty. The next day, over one hundred people were searching the mountains, looking for Rusty. They recovered a shell casing that had been fired from a rifle down close to the edge of the mountain, but there was no body to be found. Gus told the FBI he heard the shot and that he had seen a red pickup truck with Alabama license plate leaving the cabin. The FBI put out a statewide alert to find the red pickup truck. The Alabama Bureau was notified to be on the lookout for Bob.

The county sheriff's department went to Kathy's apartment to interview her to find out when was the last time she talked to Rusty. She told them about Bob coming by and what he had told her. The FBI put an APB out, looking for Bob. The police found Bob at his house in Alabama and questioned him about Rusty's disappearance. They told Bob his truck had been seen on the mountain near Rusty's cabin. They wanted to know what he was doing there. Bob told them he had gone up to the cabin to see Rusty to get permission to hunt, but Rusty was nowhere around. So he left and tried to get Kathy to go back to Alabama with him. "She wouldn't go, so I decided to come back home by myself."

He questioned Bob for several hours but didn't have enough evidence to hold him. So they return to Indian Springs to continue their investigation. The search went on for two months, and there was no sign of Rusty. The only one that knew where Rusty was, was Gus. The night that Rusty was shot, his body lay on a pile of rocks. Gus walked up and looked down at where Rusty's body was. He saw a light shining through a crack in the mountainside. A few minutes later, a door opened up and went to the side of the mountain. Two men walked out through the door and stood over Rusty's body, looking at him. They looked at each other and didn't say anything. They reached down and picked Rusty's body up and carried him inside the mountain, and the door closed behind them. Gus turned and walked away. Inside the mountain was a large opening, about the size of a football field. There was a strange bullet-shaped object sitting in the middle of the opening. The two men walked over to the ship and carried Rusty's body inside. Inside the ship was a room filled with medical equipment. They placed Rusty's body on a table and began to examine him to see what kind of damage his body had received. The bullet had entered the front of his chest and exited the back. Rusty's head had several places showing brain damage from hitting the rocks when he fell. The two men decided to save Rusty's life. They removed all the clothing and began to work on him. They had all types of medical instruments never seen by man. One man worked on the bullet wound, while the other one worked on Rusty's head.

The operation on his head was so intense; it took several days. These were not ordinary doctors, and where did they come from? After they finished repairing Rusty's body, they placed him in a sealed capsule and filled it with some type of liquid gas. He had tubes running from his mouth and threw his nose while he lay in the capsule. He was in the capsule for two weeks, and they removed him and placed him in a bed. People were still searching for Rusty as he was recovering from his injuries inside the mountain. The two doctors continued to monitor all of Rusty's vital signs for the next four days; they both agreed that he was completely healed. They set him up in a chair, and Rusty opened his eyes. The two men asked the rescue how he felt. He said, "I feel fine. Who are you? Where am I?"

The doctor said, "Come with us. We've got a lot of explaining to do."

They carried Rusty into another room that was filled with computers and electronic equipment. They asked Rusty if he was hungry.

"Yes, I would like something to eat and also something to drink."

One doctor handed Rusty a small bottle filled with a red liquid. They gave him a cup with something white that looked like ice cream and a spoon and told him to eat. "This will get your strength back and give you plenty of energy for a while."

"Okay, I feel fine now. Will you tell me who you are?"

"Okay, Rusty, we're going to tell you who we are and where we are from. We saved your life because we feel like we can trust you, and you will do what we ask you to do. We are time travelers from another world. We landed here in this mountain because it was a sacred place, and we feel like what we tell you has to be kept a secret. We come from another planet far away from here. It's a planet much like yours but millions of years older. Our technology is so far advanced from yours. We feel like your world is still living in the Stone Age. We are human beings, just like you, but much more advanced. When you fell from the mountain edge and landed in a pile of rocks, your brain was so damaged. Nobody in your world could have repaired your brain. We have so much advanced technology that we have not only repaired your brain, but the instruments that we implanted have made you hundreds of times smarter than you were before your injury.

"Your world is suffering from so many problems. We decided to save your life and give you the opportunity to help your world be a better place. You're not a superman, Rusty. You can still suffer the same problems as before. But with the knowledge we've given you, you will be able to avoid these dangers. With your knowledge, Rusty, you will be able to conquer all types of situations. You will be able to cure diseases that all of your science is not able to do. You will be able to design and build things you never thought possible. With this technology you have, you will be able to conquer a lot of the world's biggest problems. For instance, there are countries in your world where children are starving to death because they have no technology to save them. You will be able to do this. You will be able to make all the money you will ever need to do anything you want to help your planet. Rusty, we say again, all we have given you is for the good of mankind on your planet." They talked to Rusty for several days, telling him how he could use all the technology that he had now stored in his brain. With this technology, he was going to be able to solve a lot of the world's problems. They explained to him that he was never to use his technology to destroy anything on this planet. "We're going to give you this device, which is similar to your cell phone. Open it up, and speak into it, and it will record anything you want to know about your world. For example, open it up, and ask the device how many miles it is from here to Indian Springs. What did it tell you?"

"It said it was sixty-one miles."

"Now do you understand how it works?"

"Yes, I do."

"We will be leaving soon. We are returning to our world. We are going to open the door for you to leave, and we wish you the best of your world."

"I don't know who you are or where you are from, but I promise to use all this knowledge to help everyone on this planet. I will not forget you, and I want to thank you for all you have done for me."

The door opened up on the side of the mountain, and Rusty started walking and went through the door opening. Soon he reached the top of the mountain, where the cabin was. He still had the clothing that he had on when Bob shot him. The device he had been given looked just like a regular cell phone but had so much advanced technology in it. Only he knew how to work it.

Rusty sat inside the cabin for several hours, thinking how he was going to explain his disappearance. He had to keep what had happened to him a secret. How would he explain this to the woman he loved the most? Rusty was getting ready to call someone to come get him when Gus walked up.

"Hello, Rusty. I see you're doing well. Everyone has been looking for you. What are you going to tell them?"

"I don't know, Gus, but I'll come up with something."

He just turned and started walking away and said, "I know you will, Rusty."

"Goodbye, Gus. I'll see you later." Rusty called for a cab to come up to the cabin and pick him up. The cab arrived about an hour and twenty minutes later. The cabdriver said, "Are you Mr. Wilson?"

"Yes, I am."

"Everybody's been looking for you."

"I know they have, and here I am." Rusty gave the cabdriver the address of his house, and the driver carried him back to Indian Springs to where he lived. He thought about the cabdriver and walked into his house. The first thing Rusty had to do was find some more clothes to wear. He saved the clothes he had to show the police where Bob had shot him. He decided to visit Kathy first. He left his house and went over to the apartment where Kathy lived, walked up, and knocked on her door.

Kathy opened the door and saw Rusty and screamed, "Oh my god! Rusty, where have you been?" She jumped in his arms and started crying and telling him she was never going to turn him loose. Kathy said, "Everyone was thinking you were dead. We looked everywhere for you on the mountain. I almost was dead princess, but I'll tell you about it later. Right now, I just want to hold you and be close to you."

They spent about two hours holding and telling how much they had missed each other. Rusty called his office and told Sally, "I'll be there shortly, and make sure Mark and Jesse are there."

"Rusty, is this you? I'll call them right now and have them here in just a few minutes."

"Yes, it's me, Sally. I'll be there shortly."

Rusty called the police chief and asked him to be there also. Rusty and Kathy got in his truck and drove to the office. The police chief, Mark, and Jesse were all there, waiting for Rusty. Rusty and Kathy walked into the office, and everybody began jumping with excitement for seeing him again. I'm glad to be back. And if all of you will sit here, I'm going to tell you what happened and why I've been gone so long."

Everyone gathered around, and Rusty started telling the story about Bob shooting him. He told them, after Bob had shot him, two doctors had found him and started operating on him and saved his life. He didn't know who the two doctors were or where they were from, but they saved his life and kept him out until he was fully recovered. "Bob came up to the cabin and accused me of stealing his wife. He had a gun in his hand, and I tried to talk him into putting the gun down. He wouldn't listen to me. He just kept saying, 'I tried to tell you,' then he fired the gun. That's the last thing I remember. When I came to, there were two men standing over me, looking at me. They were doctors, and they had heard the gunshot. They carried me to a hospital somewhere I don't even know where it was and started repairing the gunshot wound. They kept me there until I was completely well."

The police chief told Rusty, "Now we have enough evidence to pick Bob up and charge him with attempted murder." After the meeting was over, the police chief got a warrant issued for Bob, and the state police went to Alabama to arrest Bob. The police got all the paperwork done that was needed to bring Bob back to Indian Springs. They placed Bob in the county jail, and the district attorney went to interview him. He told Bob he was being charged for attempted murder.

Bob asked, "Who am I supposed to have tried to murder?"

"You are being charged with the attempted murder of Rusty Wilson Bob."

Bob said, "I heard Rusty Wilson had disappeared!"

"We have all the evidence we need to charge you with this crime.

"Well, I want to see an attorney before you ask me any more questions."

The court appointed Bob a lawyer. They carried Bob in front of the judge and asked him how he pleaded. Bob pleaded not guilty. The judge gave him thirty days to get with his lawyer and plan out his defense. Jim Martin was Bob's attorney, and the first thing he asked Bob when they got back to the jail was, "Did you try to kill Rusty Wilson?"

Bob replied, "No, I don't know what they're talking about. I haven't tried to kill anybody."

"Bob, I'm going to see the district attorney and find out what evidence they have against you. I'll be back in a couple of days and let you know what I find out."

Jim left and went to the district attorney's office to see what kind of evidence they had against Bob.

The district attorney showed Jim the evidence he had. He had the shell casing fired from the gun that Bob owned, and the clothing that Rusty was wearing when he shot him. "We have a witness that saw Bob leaving the cabin the day Rusty was shot. You can tell your client that if he doesn't plead guilty to this, we will give him the maximum sentence the law allows if he's found guilty."

Jim thought about what the district attorney said and went back to the jail to talk to Bob. Bob's attorney sat down and told Bob, "They have a lot of evidence against you, and they are willing to make a deal. If you plead guilty, it will go easier on you."

Bob said, "I'd rather take my chance with a jury."

"If that's what you want. I will try to defend you the best I know how."

Jim called the district attorney and told him, "Bob refused to take a plea, so we are going to trial."

The police got a warrant to go to Bob's house and get the rifle that he used when he shot Rusty. They matched the shell casing with the rifle, and now they had all the evidence they needed to convict him. After two months, they went to court to try Bob for attempted murder. The district attorney offered all the evidence he had to the jury. "We also have Mr. Wilson here to testify that Bob shot him with the attempt to kill him."

They put Bob on the witness stand, and his lawyer asked him, "Did you shoot Rusty Wilson?"

"Yes," Bob answered, "I did, but it was an accident."

"What do you mean it was an accident?"

"Well, I was going to ask Rusty if I could do some deer hunting there, and I had my rifle, and it accidentally went off when I was standing there, talking to him. I didn't mean to shoot him."

"Well, what did you do after the gun went off?"

"I walked over to the edge of the mountain where he had fallen, and I didn't see him anymore. He was gone."

"Gone where?"

"I don't know where. I just looked, and he wasn't there."

After Bob finished testifying, the district attorney asked Rusty Wilson to come and sit at the stand. Rusty testified that he tried to get Bob to put the gun away, but Bob kept refusing. "He kept accusing me of stealing his wife, and the only way he could get her back would be to get rid of me. Before he fired the gun, he told me, 'I tried to tell you, Rusty, and you wouldn't listen to me.' Then he fired the gun. that's the last I remember."

The judge asked Bob's attorney, "Do you have any witnesses for your client?"

"No, Your Honor, I have none."

"Well, with that being said, I'm turning this case over to the jury."

It only took the jury thirty minutes to come back with a verdict. The judge asked the jury if they have a verdict. The jury said, "Yes, we have. We all agree that the defendant is guilty."

The judge asked Bob to stand up to hear his sentence. "Bob Ford, you have been found guilty of attempted murder, and I am here by sentencing you the maximum the law allows me to do. I hereby sentence you to forty years in the state penitentiary with no eligibility for parole." Case dismissed was ordered by the judge.

Bob looked over at Rusty and said, "You haven't seen the last of me yet."

They carried Bob out of the courtroom, and the district attorney came over to Rusty and said, "I think you'll be safe now."

Rusty and Kathy sat there in the courtroom while everybody was leaving, and Kathy said to Rusty, "We don't have to worry about him anymore, do we?"

"No, princess, you don't have to worry about him anymore."

Chapter 10

Rusty called everyone into his office and said, "I'm going to be making some changes in the company. I bought some adjoining property to the office here. I'm going to build three new buildings. One of the buildings will be for structural engineering. One of the buildings will be for medical research, and the third building will be for the legal staff that we're going to need for the expanding businesses that I'm going to have. I have bought an old bank building downtown that we're going to renovate and open up our own bank. It will be called Wilson Savings and Loan.

"I am turning all of the construction part of the company over to Mark Johnson and his brother Jesse. Kathy will be the bank president and manager of Wilson Savings and Loan. All the employees that work for us are the reason this company has grown so big. Their dedication and service has been the best I have ever seen. Starting next month, every employee will receive a bonus at the end of the year for their hard work and loyalty. This bonus will be based on the company's profits, and according to the bank records, this company has made a lot of money. The bonus that everyone's getting should be very nice. As you all know, Kathy and I will be getting married in a few days. We are getting married in Augusta, Georgia.

"Anyone that would like to attend, get with Sally, and she will make the arrangements. Does anyone have any questions? If not, I call this meeting over."

Rusty and Kathy married in Georgia and returned back to Indian Springs. They spent their honeymoon on Dogwood Mountain in the cabin. While they were at the cabin enjoying their honeymoon, Rusty was talking to Kathy about all the things he wanted to do to make the world a better place for everyone. He saw an ad on TV where the children were starving in another country, and he was going to do something about it.

"I'm going to build a farm big enough to produce enough food that no child will ever have to go hungry again. I'm going to buy all the companies that are going out of business and build them back up so all the people that work there will have good jobs, good pay, and be able to support their families the way it was intended for them to do."

Kathy told Rusty, "This is one of the reasons that I love you so much. You think more of others than you do for yourself."

"I love you, princess, and I want you to be a part of everything I do."

"I love you, Rusty, and I will always be here for you."

After spending several days in the cabin, Rusty told Kathy, "We have to go back to the village. We have a lot of work to start doing."

After returning home, Rusty went to the office and started research to find out about all the agencies that were providing food to other people.

He talked to all of them, and they said there just wasn't enough food for everyone. Rusty said to build a farm big enough to feed all the people that needed food. It was going to take a big farm. I will need a lot of land to build this farm on. Rusty decided to start searching for land to build his farm. He started looking at the world map and decided Australia would be the best place to build his ranch. Rusty got in touch with the government in Australia and told them about his plan to build a ranch. He wanted to raise food for starving people all over the world. He asked them if they had land that he could buy to build this ranch on. They told him they had thousands of acres of land that was undeveloped that they would be willing to sell. They told him the land was very dry, and he would have to look at it to see if it was good enough to build a farm. Rusty said he would like to look at this land, so he made arrangements to fly over to Australia to see this property. The governor told him he would be pleased to meet him and invited him over. "We will make arrangements for someone to meet you when you arrive here and show you the property."

Rusty told Kathy he was planning to fly to Australia to look at some property to build a farm and ranch on. "I will keep in touch with you every day and let you know how it's going."

"Are you sure you don't want me to go with you. Rusty?"

"No, princess, you need to stay with the bank. I may have to have money transferred to the land agency in Australia. I will need you to take care of that for me when the time comes. It's a nine-thousand-mile trip from here to Sydney, Australia, and will take more than sixteen hours. I may be gone for at least one or two weeks. I will keep in touch with you every day." Rusty packed all the things he was going to need to make the trip and left the next morning. He arrived in Sydney twenty hours later. When he arrived at the airport, Desi was sitting there, waiting for him.

"Welcome to Australia, Mr. Wilson!"

"Thank you, Desi. You can call me Rusty."

"Come with me to the state house. That's where you will be staying while you're here." Desi told Rusty to get settled in his room. "And I will come by around seven o'clock to pick you up. We will go to dinner, and after that we will go to my office and show you some maps of the land that we are willing to sell."

They spent several hours in Desi's office, looking at maps. Rusty said, "I will be back tomorrow, and we will talk some more. Right now, I need to get some rest after the long trip."

The next day, Rusty went back to Desi's office, and they talked more about the land he was going to look at. Rusty picked out one piece of property and asked Desi if he could get an aircraft where they could fly over the land to look at it first.

"Yes, Rusty, I can have a plane ready in about two hours."

While Rusty was waiting for the plane, he called Kathy and told her everything was going well in Sydney. They talked for a while, and Rusty told her he would be getting in touch with her later on in the afternoon.

"I love you, Rusty, and I'll be waiting for your call."

"I love you too, princess, and I will talk to you later."

That morning, Rusty boarded a helicopter and traveled four hours to reach the property they were looking at. The property they were looking at was located 208 miles from Sydney. It was mostly flat land and very dry. There was a mountain located east of the property, and Rusty wanted to fly over it and check it out. There was a small stream of water running between the mountain, and Rusty said, "If I could build a dam here in this valley, there would be enough water to irrigate the land and make it possible to have a ranch."

Desi said, "The mountain is included in this track of land."

They traveled all day, looking at the property. The property was estimated to be eighty square miles. Rusty told Desi, "I think this piece of property is exactly what I'm looking for. Let's go back to your office and see if we can make a deal on it."

After they returned to the office, they got all the paperwork ready and agreed on a price. Rusty agreed to pay $80 million for the property. He agreed to have the money there the next day. That night, Rusty called Kathy and told her about the land he was buying and to send him a bank draft for $80 million. The next day, the money arrived, and Rusty paid for the land. Rusty told Desi he was leaving to go back to the US. He would be back in about a month to start work on building the farm. Rusty left the next morning, and as soon as he arrived, he started making plans for what he was going to need to get the ranch and farm started. He needed to open up a banking account in Sydney to pay for all the construction that he would be doing on the property.

He got with his best engineers and told them they would be going to Australia to build a dam on the property he had purchased. The engineers were all excited about going and would be glad to do all they could for his project. Rusty told the engineers it would be several days before he could get with them and make the final arrangements to leave for Sydney. Late that afternoon, Rusty and Kathy were having dinner at their house, and Rusty asked Kathy, "Why are you looking so down? You just don't look happy for some reason, princess?"

"Why should I be happy? You're planning on leaving me for who knows how long in a foreign land."

"I won't be gone that long, princess. As soon as I get a place for us to stay on the property, you will be able to fly over there with me. Once I get everybody lined up on what they have to do, I'll be flying back here. I'm not going to leave you for any long period at a time. We're going to get someone to take your place at the bank, and you will be able to travel with me anytime and anywhere I go."

"Well, that makes me feel better, Rusty. I just miss you too much when you're not around."

"I feel the same way about you, princess. Let us not worry about it right now. Let's enjoy the rest of the afternoon."

A few days after, Rusty and the engineering crew got ready to leave for Australia. They left Indian Springs and arrived in Sydney the next day. When Rusty arrived in Sydney, he opened up a banking account with one of the local banks. He went to one of the employment offices and told the manager he would be hiring a lot of help for his projects. They agreed to give him all the help he needed. He got with one of the heavy equipment companies and made a deal with them to furnish all the heavy equipment he would need to build his ranch. Rusty got with one of the local contractors and asked if he would be willing to build a house on the property for all the people that would be working on the project. The contractor agreed to build anything he wanted and was ready to start at any time. The contractor notified all the building suppliers and let them know that he would be needing a lot of material. They agreed to supply him with anything he needed.

As soon as the contractor got the first house built, Rusty was going to send his engineering crew to start planning on building a dam between the mountains. As soon as the engineers had a place to live, they would start designing the dam. The engineers would have the dam built big enough to supply water for the entire property as well as power. The dam would have two large generators in it to supply the power. Rusty was well pleased with the design that they came up with and asked them to get started as soon as possible building the dam. Men and supplies were arriving every day. Heavy equipment was brought in to start building the dam. All kinds of buildings were being built for storing supplies. It wouldn't be long before the place started looking like a small town. Rusty had one of his banking employees fly over to Sydney and take care of all his banking. They would be in charge of making payroll for all the people he had working. Everything seemed to be going good on the project, and Rusty told his head engineer he was leaving tomorrow to go back to the US. I've got several things I've got to do once I get back home.

"If you need anything, let me know. I will be back over here in a month or so. Keep in touch with me, and let me know how the project's going." Rusty left the next day going back to the US. Once he arrived at the airport, Kathy was standing there, waiting on him. She was so excited to see Rusty again. They embraced each other for a few minutes and then went home later that night. Kathy told Rusty she would like to go up and spend a few days at the cabin. He told her that sounded like a great idea. They would go up tomorrow and spend a few days. The next morning, they left for the cabin. They spent the day enjoying the beautiful mountain, and late that afternoon, they heard a sound coming from the Indian burial ground. He told Kathy, "Come with me. We're going to visit the burial ground."

When they got there, Gus was standing inside the burial site. "Hello, Gus. How are you doing?"

"I have been doing well, Rusty. Who is this pretty lady?"

"Yes, this is my wife, Kathy. I call her princess."

"Well, I agree with you, Rusty. She looks like a princess."

"Thank you, guys, for the compliment. Do you come here often?"

"Yes, I come here about once every day. This place is guarded by the spirits."

"This is a beautiful place, Gus. And if there are spirits here, I know they are well pleased."

"Yes, Mrs. Wilson, I know they are well also."

"Gus, it is good seeing you, but Kathy and I have to be headed home."

On the way home, Kathy asked Rusty, "What did Gus mean when he said the spirits would be well pleased?"

"Well, princess, Gus thanks this place is guarded by spirits from the Native Americans. Sometimes I believe they are spirits around the burial site."

"Well, I hope they're good spirits, Rusty."

"They are, princess. You don't have anything to worry about."

Chapter 11

Kathy's birthday was coming up, and Rusty decided to go shopping and buy her a ring. While he was walking through the mall, he noticed a man had been following him. Everywhere he went, he noticed this man was always within sight of him. He decided to find out who it was. He saw a police officer standing at the entrance of the shoe store and walked up to him.

"Hello, Officer. I was wondering if you could help me out."

"Help you out with what, sir?"

"My name is Rusty Wilson, and there's a man following me all over this mall. I would like for you to walk up to him with me and find out who he is."

"Where is this man?" the police officer asked.

"He's standing down there by that booth in the middle of the mall where they sell cell phones. He has a gray suit on and a black hat."

"I see the man you're talking about, and you say he's been following you"

"Yes, he has been following me, and he has someone else with him, I think. There's another man over in the jewelry store I think is with him."

"Well, let's walk down there and see who he is."

Rusty and the police officer walked down to where the man was standing, and the officer asked him for his ID.

"Why do you want to see my ID, Officer?"

"This man says you have been following him, and he wants to know who you are. So if you will show me your ID…"

The man pulled out his identification and showed it to the police officer. His name was William Clark. He was an agent for the FBI.

"Why is the FBI following this man?"

"I really can't tell, Officers. It is confidential information, and I'm not allowed to discuss it with anyone other than my boss."

"What about your partner that's working with you? Can you have him come over here?"

William turned and looked at the man standing in the jewelry store and motioned for him to come over. The man came out of the jewelry store and walked over to where Rusty and the police officer were standing. William asked him to show his badge to the police officer. The police officer took his badge and looked at it and said, "Your name is Larry Cork?"

"Yes, sir, it is."

"Well, Mr. Wilson, now you know who these two gentlemen are, and what are you going to do about them following you?"

"Well, Officer, I appreciate you coming down here with me and finding out who these two men are."

"Well, Mr. Wilson, I will leave you in good hands with these two FBI agents." The police officer turned and walked away.

Rusty told the two FBI agents he would like to find out more about what they were doing with him. He invited them down to a coffee shop located at the end of the mall. "If you will go with me, I'll buy you a cup of coffee, and I will tell you anything you want to know about me."

The two agents agreed to walk down to the coffee shop with Rusty. They went in and sat down. Rusty sat there for a few minutes, looking at the two men, and said, "I know who you are. I don't know what you're after, so maybe you can tell me?"

"We are not allowed to discuss what we do with anyone other than our boss."

"I know who your boss is, and tell him what I'm offering to pay you and see if he's okay with you retiring from your job with the government. His name is Edward Burns. He is the chief investigator in the Nashville office."

"How is it that you know my boss?"

"I have my own ways of investigating people. It will only take me a few minutes to find out everything I want to know about the two of you. How long have you been working with the FBI, William?"

"Why do you want to know about me, Mr. Wilson?"

"Call me Rusty. We don't have to be so formal. If you've been with the FBI more than twenty years, I think it's time you retired. I would like for you to go to work for me. I need two good men that are willing to investigate people that I need to know more about. I will pay you double whatever the government is paying you. I want you two men to ask your boss and tell him what I'm offering to pay you and see if he's okay with you retiring from your job with the government. I'm going to give you my phone number. And when you meet with him, if he wants to meet with me, I will be glad to come in and talk to him."

Rusty and the two agents sat in the coffee shop and talked for about two hours. Rusty told them all about the benefits he was willing to give them if they would come to work for him. When they left the coffee shop, William and Larry told Rusty they would get in touch with him. When William and Larry got to their car and sat there, they talked to each other for about twenty minutes.

"You know, Rusty Wilson is a very wealthy man, and the job he's offering us might not be a bad job. Let's go to our home office and talk to Mr. Burns and see what he thinks about this."

Rusty continued to shop in the mall and found a ring he bought for Kathy and several other things he was going to give her for her birthday. Kathy was no longer working at the bank, and now she was working as Rusty's private secretary. They hired a new bank manager to take Kathy's place so she and Rusty would be closer to each other while working. When Rusty got back to the office, he told Kathy about the two FBI agents and the conversation he had with them.

"Why would the FBI be following you, Rusty?"

"I don't know, but we're soon going to find out."

Two weeks had passed since Rusty had talked to the FBI agents. The phone rang at Kathy's desk, and it was the FBI agent William Cork.

"I would like to speak to Rusty Wilson please."

Kathy walked into Rusty's office and told him that William Clark was on the line, waiting to talk to him.

"Thank you, princess. I was waiting to hear from them."

"Hello. This is Rusty Wilson. What can I do for you?"

Rusty, this is William Clark. My partner and I have been thinking about the offer you made us in the coffee shop! We talked to our boss, and he wants you to come in and talk to all of us about the offer you made."

"I will be glad to do that, William. When would you like for me to come in?"

"He would like for you to come in tomorrow, if that's possible."

"I will be glad to come in tomorrow. What time would you like for me to be there?"

"One in the afternoon, if that's okay with you."

"That's fine with me, William. I'll be there around one o'clock tomorrow afternoon."

Rusty asked Kathy to come into his office, and he told her he was going to fly down to Nashville and meet with the FBI agent that he had met in the coffee shop. "They want me to meet with their boss and talk about going to work for us. So I'm going down there tomorrow. Would you like to go with me?"

"Do you want me to go with you, Rusty?"

"Yes, princess, you can go. And after the meeting, we will spend a little time in Nashville. We can visit an old friend of mine there that I haven't seen in quite a while."

"You mean Becky?"

"Yes, Becky is the one person I'm thinking about. I have another friend there that owns a steel mill that we rebuilt for him, and we own a small part of the business."

The next day, Rusty and Kathy flew to Nashville. They got a taxi to take them to the Federal Building. They walked in the building and asked to see the director of the FBI. They were told to go to the elevator and go up to the fifth floor, and someone would direct them to the director's office. They got off the elevator and walked over to the receptionist's desk and asked to see Mr. Burns. The lady got up from her desk and said, "Follow me," and walk down the hall. She opened the door and said, "Mr. Burns, there's a Mr. Wilson here to see you."

Rusty and Kathy walked into Mr. Burns's office.

"I'm Rusty Wilson, and this is my wife, Kathy. I have an appointment to talk to you about your agents."

"Yes, I know, Mr. Wilson. I will call William and Larry to come into my office, if you don't mind. I would like for your wife to wait outside with the receptionist."

Rusty turned and took Kathy back out the door and asked her to stay with the receptionist. Kathy sat down and started talking to the receptionist.

"I guess they have something to talk about. They don't want me in there."

"Yes," the reception said, "he doesn't like anyone in the room except the people he's dealing with. It's nothing against you, Mrs. Wilson."

"Oh, I'm okay with that."

A few minutes later, William and Larry walked by and went into Mr. Burns's office. William and Larry shook hands with Rusty and said, "We're glad to see you again, Rusty."

Mr. Burns told everybody to have a seat. "Now let's talk about the offer you made to my two best agents. You want them to retire and go to work for you, is that right?"

"Yes, sir, I offered them a job to go to work for me. I plan to use them as my personal bodyguards and do investigative work for me. I have done a background check on these two men and like what I have learned. I feel like they can be trusted with anything I have going on in my business."

"How is it, Mr. Wilson., that you know so much about these two agents? I've been telling you no more about them than I do."

"I have my own way of getting information about people. It's a technique that I learned several years ago that I want to keep to myself. If I have to, I will teach William and Larry a lot of my investigative techniques. Maybe someday the FBI will learn some of these ways to investigate. I know you have done a lot of investigations on me, Mr. Burns. You know who I am and where I'm from. I am open with everything I do. If there's anything I have that you want to know about, I will be glad to tell you. There's a lot of things that I want to do to make this world a better place to live. I'm making a lot of money, and I want to use that money to make this a better life for everybody that I come in contact with. I don't intend to harm anyone in my adventures that I am working for. I work hard, and I work smart. My grandfather told me, when I was just a kid, he said you are one of the smartest kids I've ever known. If you always use that good 'for all mankind,' you will wind up being one of the richest men in the world and will be honored for all your kindness."

"Well, we have done a lot of investigative work on you, Mr. Wilson, not only by Will and Larry but our other agents across the country. We know you were shot at one time and are proud that you survived the ordeal. I believe that you are honest and a good person. Therefore I'm telling Will and Larry, if they want to go to work for you, they would be making a good choice for them and their families. They can retire anytime they get ready to, and I wish them both the best of luck."

Rusty turned and looked at Will and Larry and told them, "If you decide you want to go to work for me, you have my number and know where my office is. I will welcome you anytime" Rusty stood up and told Mr. Burns he wouldn't take any more of his time, and it was a pleasure meeting him. Rusty said goodbye to Will and Larry and walked out the door. He got to the reception desk and told Kathy, "The meeting is over. Now let's go see if we can find some place to have a good dinner."

They walked over to the elevator and left the building. They went to the Grand Hotel, where they were planning on spending the night and had a good dinner in a restaurant. After the dinner, Rusty told Kathy, "Let's ride down and visit my friend Becky."

Kathy said, "Let's go. I would be glad to meet her."

They drove downtown to the hotel and bar at Becky Owens's. When they got there, Becky was behind the bar. And when she saw Rusty walk in, she jumped with joy. "Oh, I'm so excited to see you, Rusty. And how have you been?"

"I've been doing great, Becky. I want you to meet my wife. This is Kathy. Kathy, this is Becky and an old friend of mine."

Becky said, "I am so pleased to meet you, Kathy. I have heard a lot of good things about you."

"Thank you, Becky. Rusty has told me a lot about you and him growing up together and how good a friend you were."

"I'm so happy for you, Kathy. You have the best man you could ever have wished for."

"Thank you, Becky. I know, and I love him more than anything in the world."

"Come and sit down, Rusty and Kathy. We've got a lot to catch up on."

They sat there for several hours, talking to each other.

"Rusty, how long are you and Kathy going to be in Nashville?"

"We plan to leave tomorrow morning. We have a lot of work to do back home, but we will be dropping in on you every once in a while."

They said goodbye to Becky and left and went back to the hotel. They spent the night and left the next morning, going back to Indian Springs.

On the way home, Kathy asked Rusty what kind of relationship he had with Becky growing up. He told her, "We were the best of friends, and there was nothing I wouldn't do for her. That's the kind of friend she is."

The next day was Kathy's birthday, and after dinner, he gave her the ring that he had purchased in the mall. He handed her the ring and said, "Happy birthday, princess. I love you more than anything in the world."

The ring was heart-shaped and had several ruby stones around the heart.

"Rusty, that ring is beautiful. I love it and love you so much, darling."

The next day, at the office, Rusty told Kathy all about the meeting he had with the FBI director, and he was hoping that the two men, William and Larry, would come to work for him.

"If they come to work here, I'm going to put them in the office down the hall. They will be more or less my bodyguards and will do special investigative work I want done. They will be two men that I put a lot of trust in, and they will be looking out for me and you, princess."

"Do you think you're going to have trouble, Rusty?"

"No, I don't think so, but I want to be ready if we do."

Two weeks passed, and William and Larry called Rusty and told him they were coming down to go to work for him. "We are bringing our families with us and would like you to help us find a place to live."

Rusty told them he already had two new houses for them to move into. "I believe your families will really like living here."

When they arrived in Indian Springs, the houses were ready for them to move their families in, and they were ready to go to work. Rusty brought them to the office and showed them where their office would be, just down the hall from his. "Let me know whatever you need to get settled in, and then I will bring you up to date on everything."

They were introduced to all the people working in the office, and they told everyone how proud they were to be here. Rusty called Mark and Jesse to come to his office. He told them he had hired ex–FBI agents to go to work with him. He told Mark, "We are starting a lot of new businesses and are going to need to hire a lot of new employees. William and Larry will be in charge of doing all the background checks on all the people that we are planning on hiring."

Rusty called Will and Larry to come to his office. When they got there, he introduced them to Mark and Jesse. Mark said, "Welcome aboard. We'll be glad to work with you."

They all shook hands and went back to their offices.

Rusty called for a special meeting two weeks after William and Larry started to work with him. All the office personnel would be at the meeting. He started out by saying, "Will and Larry will be doing most of our security work, and that work requires doing a lot of traveling. I'm going to ask everyone here to go with me and start learning how to fly the company plane. We all need to know how to fly the plane because we are going to do a lot of traveling in the coming months. We will have the company pilot to teach each one of us how to fly the plane. As soon as we have our license to fly, we will be able to go places if the pilot we have is not available to go. I know I'm going to enjoy flying a plane on my own, and I'm sure you will too. Next week, we will all begin taking our flying lessons. Is everyone here willing to do that?"

Everyone agreed they like the idea of learning how to fly. Rusty, Mark, Jesse, Larry, and William all started their flying lessons. They went to school for three hours every afternoon. The teacher that was teaching them in the classroom walked over to Rusty and said, "Can I talk to you in my office for a minute, please?"

Rusty said yes, and they both walked into the office. The teacher told Rusty to sit down.

"I want to talk to you for a minute about the classes you all are taking. Everyone is doing good in class except for you! It's like you already know everything in the book. Have you studied flying before?"

"Just between me and you, I don't have to take lessons to know how to fly. I don't want my people to know that I already know how to fly. So I decided to take the lessons with them. I will be able to help them in the future when we get our own planes. I would appreciate it if you would keep this conversation private!"

"I will be glad to do that, Rusty, and I will appreciate all the help you can give me and teaching these guys how to fly."

As the weeks went by, everyone was learning how to fly in the classroom. Now it was time to take to the air. Rusty said, "I'll go first."

Rusty and the instructor boarded the plane and took off down the runway. The instructor sat there and watched Rusty as the plane left the ground. They flew all around for about twenty minutes, and the instructor said, "Take it back in. You already know how to fly better than I do."

"Well, I appreciate you saying that. I guess I can find other things to do while you're teaching the rest of the guys."

With Rusty's help, after a few weeks, everybody received their pilot's license. Rusty had a meeting at the office and told Mark, "We're going to have our own planes. And whenever you all need to fly somewhere, you can go without hesitation."

The company was getting so big now and going worldwide. Rusty was hiring more and more people to run his businesses. After a year had passed, Rusty called a meeting for all the people that were running different parts of the businesses. He said, "I want to let everyone know, you are all doing a great job. I'm not going to be in the office for a while. I'm planning to do a lot of traveling in the next couple of years. All of you will be running the entire business. If you need me, I will always be as close as your phone."

After the meeting was over, Rusty and Kathy left to spend a few days at the cabin in the mountain. While they were at the cabin, they were deciding where they wanted to travel, and they spent several days enjoying the weather. It was springtime, and all the dogwoods were in bloom.

"Do you know, princess, I don't think there's any place in the world more beautiful than right here. I think, when I bought this place, I was reborn again."

"You are right, Rusty. I think this is just a little bit of heaven here on earth. They spent the rest of the day walking around and looking at the dogwood trees.

"It's easy to see why, princess, they call this place Dogwood Mountain." When they left the cabin and went back home, they packed their suitcases, ready to travel. The first place they decided to go was Australia to visit the ranch that Rusty had built. The next day, they headed to Australia. When they arrived in Sydney, they took a small plane and flew out to the ranch. The ranch had its own landing strip for small planes. The ranch was supplying enough food products to feed all the less fortunate people that didn't have anything to eat in Africa and other surrounding countries. Rusty told Kathy, "The ranch is selling enough food products to keep the ranch going without costing the company any money. This is one of the best investments we have ever made."

After spending several weeks in Australia, they left and flew to Europe.

They spent time in Germany, France, Italy, and several other countries. After spending a year abroad, they flew back to the United States. After returning home, Rusty called for a board meeting with all the people that was running his business.

"The reason I call for this board meeting is I would like to discuss a new idea that I have. As you all know, we now have more than two hundred thousand employees. You and all these employees are the reason this company is so big. I want to give back to the employees of this company. What I would like to do is find some land and build a place where all the employees could go and spend their vacation without any cost to them. I was thinking, maybe a resort area that would have all types of entertainment that any employee would enjoy. For instance, I would like to build a place with a golf course, swimming, boating, and fishing; a restaurant, where they could eat without any cost; a hotel, where they could spend their nights. I want this to be a place for the entire family to spend time together and have fun without any cost to them. We will provide transportation to and from this resort to all employees at no cost. It is my belief that the employees of this company are the ones that have made this company what it is today. Therefore, by building this place, I would like to show them my appreciation for all their hard work. I will let everyone know, when I find some land that I like, I want this land to be convenient for everyone that works for us. I want to thank everyone for coming to this meeting, and I will be seeing you later."

Rusty stood up, and everyone started clapping their hands. After everyone left the meeting, Mark walked up to Rusty and said, "This is why I came to work for you. They don't make them any better than you are, Rusty."

"Thank you, Mark. That's why I hired you and Jesse. I knew the two of you could make this company all I had ever dreamed it would be."

They shook hands, and Mark walked away.

Chapter 12

Rusty told Kathy, "We are going to start traveling all over the US and see if we can find a good place to build a resort for the employees."

"Where do you want to go first?"

"I was thinking we would fly out west somewhere, princess."

"I would love to do that, Rusty. When are we leaving?"

"Whenever you tell me you're ready, princess, we will go."

Kathy started packing their suitcases and getting everything they needed for their travel. They left Indian Springs the next day, traveling west, and they visited Arizona, Wyoming, North and South Dakota, Utah, and Nevada. They spent several weeks in each state and decided any one of these states would be a good place to build. After they got back home, Rusty started the process of financial property. He had real estate people all over each one of the states, looking for some property to build on. After going over all the pieces of property that people had sent him, he received one piece that really caught his attention. There was a tract of land that belonged to a mining company that had gone out of business. It was a forty thousand acres located sixty miles northeast of Las Vegas, Nevada. He told Kathy, "This sounds like it might be the place we're looking for."

Kathy said, "Okay, Rusty, I'll pack a few things, and we'll fly out there and check it out."

The next day, they were on their way to Nevada to check out the property. "While we're there, why don't we spend a few days in Las Vegas and have some fun, princess?"

"I would love to do that, Rusty. I have never been there before."

"Do you think we should leave our money at home, princess?"

"I don't know, Rusty. You've been really lucky so far. You met me, didn't you?"

"Yes, princess, I was lucky when I met you. You have filled all the emptiness that I had in my life." After arriving in Las Vegas, they spent a few days there and decided to check out the land that was for sale. They met with a real estate agent and drove down to where the property was. They rode around for several hours, looking at some of the property, and Rusty said, "I would like to rent a plane and fly over the property."

The agent agreed that would be a good thing to do. So they drove back to Las Vegas and agreed to meet the next day.

They rented a helicopter to fly over the land and get a better view. They flew over all the property the next day, and Rusty said, "This is where I want to build the resort area."

Now all he needed was to agree on a price for the property. Rusty met with the owners the next day, and they all agreed on a price. Rusty went to the bank and got a bank draft for the money, and he sat down with the owners. They signed all the necessary paperwork, and now the property belonged to Rusty. The next day, Rusty and Kathy flew back home, and Rusty went to work immediately, planning out his resort area. He got with his engineers and said, "I want the ones that built the ranch in Australia to design and build a resort area in Nevada."

Rusty gave them pictures and maps of the area, and they started to design what was going to be one of the finest resort areas in the country. After several months of design work, a group of engineers flew out to Nevada to set up a workstation. Rusty went to the county seat and gave them maps of what they were going to build. The county inspectors said they would issue permits for each building they were going to build, and they would have to inspect them as they were being built. Rusty agreed to set up a temporary office for the county inspectors. The office would be located next door to the engineering office. Rusty told his chief engineer he was flying back to the valley. "Keep me in touch with how everything's going." Some of the officials were wondering if this was going to be another gambling spot since it was so close to Las Vegas. Rusty assured them that this was going to be a resort area for his employees only. Some of the state officials had close ties with the casinos, and they decided to stop Rusty's project. They had a court hearing to see if they could stop the project, but the court ruled. Rusty had not violated any law and would be able to continue building his resort. The estimated cost for building the resort was over two billion dollars. The engineers estimated the project would be complete in two years. While the resort was being built, Rusty was spending more time at Indian Springs. His construction business was getting bigger and bigger and soon would be the largest construction company in America. He would now be the second richest man in the world.

Chapter 13

A lady walked in the construction office late one afternoon and asked to speak to Rusty Wilson. The receptionist asked her, "What's your name, and why do you need to see Mr. Wilson?"

She said, "My name is Mary Stone, and this is my son, Jeremiah. I want to talk to him about his private life. Mrs. Stone, if you will have a seat over there, I will see if Mr. Wilson's in. The receptionist walked into Kathy's office and said, "Mrs. Stone would like to speak to Rusty. I asked her why, and she said it was something personal."

"Tell her someone will be with her in a few minutes."

Kathy got up and walked into Rusty's office and said, "There's a lady outside who would like to speak to you. She wouldn't tell the receptionist what she wanted, so would you like for me to bring her in here?"

"Yes, princess. I'll talk to her. Kathy walked out to the lobby and told the lady, "Mr. Wilson will see you now." She walked the lady to Rusty's office. "Come into my office, Mrs. Stone, and have a seat. Mary said this is my son, Jeremiah, and I wanted to see if you could help him."

"What do you mean to help him?"

"I have carried him to every doctor in the state, and they all tell me the same thing. My son has a rare disease, and they tell me nothing can be done. They are only giving him three months to live. I was told by a friend of mine who works for your company that you have a research center and may be able to help my son. We do have a medical research center here and have been able to come up with medicine to help a lot of illnesses."

"How old is your son?"

"He will be four years old next month."

"What kind of illness did they say he had?"

"They said it was a type of leukemia that was very rare, and they had no cure for it. I don't know what we can do for your son, Mrs. Stone, but I will go to the building and talk to some of my research people and see what we can do. I don't want to give you any false hope, Mrs. Stone. All I can tell you is that we will try to find something to help your son. What I want you to do is go down to our research center and let them take a sample of your son's blood, and we will go from there."

Mrs. Stone carried her son down to the research center, and they took several samples of blood from him. They told her to take her son home, and they would keep in touch and let her know if they had anything that might help. The next day, Rusty went over to the research center and was talking to the person in charge of the research. He asked him, "Have y'all tested the blood of the young boy that came in here yesterday?"

"Yes, sir, we have run eight tests on the blood so far, and we don't have anything that we can find will help him. We will keep working on our mixture of chemicals to see if we can find something."

Rusty said, "I want to save this kid's life. We have got to find something to help him. Keep working on it, and I'll get back with you tomorrow. I'm going to do some research myself."

All day and up until the night, Rusty was searching through thousands of plants to see if he could come up with something. Kathy walked into his office and said, "Are you going to work all night, Rusty?"

"I don't know, princess. But if I have to, I will."

Later on that night, Rusty discovered a plant that was growing in the Everglades of Florida. It had a chemical on the root of the plant that Rusty felt that might be the answer. The next day, Rusty had someone send him some of the plants growing in the Everglades. The plants arrived that afternoon, and Rusty carried them over to the lab. He told the chemists to take the roots and mix the chemical with the other ingredients that they had come up with. They told

Rusty they needed some more blood from the young boy because they had to use all the samples up. Rusty got Kathy to call Mary and tell her to bring her son back to the lab. They needed more blood. Mary brought her son back, and they took more blood. She asked the chemist if they had found anything that would help. The chemist told her they had found a drug that would slow the disease down but was not a cure. "We have one more ingredient that we're going to try, and hope that it will help."

The chemist mixed the chemical from the plant that they had received from Florida with the other chemicals and tested it on Jeremiah's blood. The results were positive. It had completely killed the virus that was in Jeremiah's blood. Everyone in the lab started celebrating. They called Rusty and told him the good news. Rusty called Mary and told her to bring her son; he had great news to tell her.

Mary brought her son in and sat down with Rusty.

"Mary, I have to tell you we have a drug that killed bacteria in Jeremiah's blood. I also have to tell you that the FDA has not tested this drug. We can give your son some of the drug but only at your request."

"Are you saying this drug will cure my son and save his life?"

"I can only tell you, Mary, that the test we made destroyed the bacteria in your son's blood that was causing the illness. It is totally up to you if we give him this drug."

"Yes, Mr. Wilson, give him the drug." Mary carried Jeremiah into the room where they gave him the shot. They told Mary to take him home and bring him back the next day. Mary carried Jeremiah home that afternoon. When she got up the next morning to bring him back to the lab, he looked like a different person. He had the biggest smile you could have ever seen. Tears were rolling down Mary's eyes, for she knew her son had been saved. She carried him back to the lab, and they tested his blood again. There was no leukemia in his blood. The lab tech called Rusty and told him the good news. Rusty said, "I will be right over." Rusty and Kathy arrived at the lab, and Mary ran up to Rusty and gave him the biggest hug anybody had ever given.

Kathy told Mary, "God has given Rusty and these men the ability to save your son's life. We all have to thank God for this miracle."

After the celebration was over, Rusty called the drug manufacturer that he had been dealing with and told them he had a new drug that he wanted to sell them. "It's a cure for a rare leukemia, and I want the world to be able to get the use of it."

The drug company got the sample and tested it and agreed to buy it. The FDA was given a sample of it, and they also approved it for sale. Once again, the brain power that Rusty was given when he was injured had proven to be super good. As time would pass, Rusty's chemical lab would be world-renowned. They had solved many life-threatening diseases that existed in the world. Some people wanted Rusty to receive the Nobel Peace prize, but he rejected, saying, "There are other people that deserve it more than I do."

Chapter 14

Several months had passed, and Rusty was sitting at his desk, looking at a new project he was thinking about building, when Kathy walked in.

"There are two men in the lobby who would like to speak to you, Rusty. They said they were from the White House."

"Thank you, princess, for bringing them in."

Kathy went and got the two men and brought them into Rusty's office. They showed Rusty their ID and said they were from the state department.

"We have a subpoena here to give you. You are to appear before the judiciary committee on February 1 of this year." They handed Rusty the papers and turned and walked out of the building. Rusty sat down at his desk and started reading the paper. The paper said he had to appear in front of the senate on February the first. That gave Rusty only two weeks to find out what was going on with this subpoena. Kathy walked back into Rusty's office and asked him what was going on with the White House. Rusty replied, "I don't know, but I've only got two weeks to find out. Call William and Larry and have them come into my office as soon as they can."

Kathy called William and Larry and told them Rusty wanted to see them in his office as soon as possible. William and Larry soon arrived at Rusty's office, and he told them about the subpoena he had to go before the senate. "I want you two men to start investigating and find out what's going on. I will need the information as soon as you can get it!"

Two days later, William and Larry came back to Rusty's office and sat down and said, "This is what we found out: We talked with the senator from Tennessee, and he said that two senators from Nevada have filed a complaint that you may have violated antitrust laws."

"That's why you have to go before the senate. We investigated the two senators from Nevada and found out they have ties with the casino in Las Vegas. We found out that one of the senators has been taking money from the casino. We have some contacts that are working on both of the senators to give us more information."

"William, I want you to make sure that you have all the information you can get recorded and documented so I can take it to the hearing!"

"Are you going to take your lawyers with you, Rusty?"

"No William, I want you and Larry to go with me and make sure you keep me updated on what you're finding out. I know every law that has been written on antitrust, and I have never violated any of these laws. This is a witch hunt, and these senators are trying to make me look bad. You two go back to work, and I'm going to start preparing for my defense."

It was two days before Rusty had to go before the senate. Rusty started going over all the information that William and Larry had gotten him. Rusty had information that the two senators were taking money from the casino. They also were being paid hush money for state contracts they were involved with. With all the information Rusty had on the two senators, it looked like they may be the two going to jail. The day finally came when Rusty had to appear before the senate. Rusty walked into the chamber with Larry and William. The master of arms showed Rusty where they would be seated. They sat there for about thirty minutes while all the members were coming in. There was twelve senators, plus the chairman, sitting in front of Rusty. The chairman asked Rusty and the two men with him to stand and identify themselves. After telling the chairman who they were, they were asked to take the oath and be sworn in. The chairman called for the meeting to begin. He said, "This meeting is to determine whether or not Rusty Wilson has violated antitrust laws. Each senator will have five minutes to question the accused. I would like to remind everyone that this is not a trial, only an investigation. Mr. Wilson is not on trial here. We are here only to find out if there have been any laws broken. We will start this hearing by giving the senator from Nevada five minutes to question Mr. Wilson."

"Mr. Wilson, it has been brought to my attention that you intend on building a casino in the state of Nevada without the approval of the state, therefore you have violated antitrust laws."

Rusty asked the chairman, "Where is the proof that I'm building a casino? The senator from Nevada will answer that question."

"Is it not true, Mr. Wilson, that you are spending millions of dollars to build a resort area not more than fifty miles from Las Vegas?"

"That is true, Senator. It is a resort, and it's being built for my employees to spend their vacations if they so desire. It's not a place to gamble. If they decide they want to gamble, then they have the right to go to Las Vegas. Mr. Chairman, I would like to speak to everyone here in the chamber, if I may, sir?"

"You have the floor, Mr. Wilson. What is it you would like to talk about?"

"These two gentlemen sitting here beside me or private investigators, they once worked for the FBI but retired and came to work for me. When I heard about coming before the senate with some ridiculous idea that I had violated antitrust laws, I decided to do some investigations of my own. I was told the two senators from Nevada are the ones making the charges against me. So I decided to investigate the two senators. Through my investigation, I have found out and have documented proof that the two senators have been taking money from the casinos and putting it in a secret banking account in the Cayman Islands. These banking accounts have large sums of money, which have never been reported. I have three other sources where the senators have been extorting money."

One of the senators from Nevada stood up and said, "Mr. Chairman, are we going to sit here and listen to these unfounded accusations against me and my colleague?"

Rusty spoke up. "Mr. Chairman, what I'm telling you here about the senators is documented facts. Before coming to this meeting this morning, I turned these records over to the FBI. I talked to the director, and he assured me that warrants would be issued for these two senators."

There began an uproar in the chamber, and the chairman called for a recess. "We will return after a fifteen-minute recess."

All the senators started leaving the chamber, and Rusty was asked to remain in his seat until they returned. After the fifteen-minute recess, all these senators and the chairman return, except for the two senators from Nevada. After everyone was seated, the chairman called for the meeting to begin. The chairman began speaking.

"Everyone is here, except the two senators from Nevada. The reason they're not here is because the FBI had warrants for their arrest when they walked out of the chamber. They were put in handcuffs and carried away. Is there anyone here in the chamber who would like to speak?"

"Yes, Mr. Chairman, I would like to say a few words, if I may."

"The senator from Tennessee has the floor. You shall speak now, sir."

"Mr. Chairman, I would like to speak on behalf of Mr. Wilson from whom I have known for a long time. This man started a construction business when he was eighteen years old in Indian Springs, Tennessee. This company he owns has grown to be the largest construction company in the world. He has done more good for this country and especially for the state of Tennessee than anybody I have ever known. He has a ranch in Australia that he built to raise food for people that have none. He does not charge one penny for this food that he gives away. He has the most loyal employees of any company working today, and the reason why is because of the way he treats his employees. He's building a resort area for his employees so they can spend their vacation at no cost to them. They are some of the highest paid employees in the market today. They have more benefits than any company has ever offered any employee. This man's business has been built on honesty and integrity. That's why he has been so successful. These accusations that were brought here today against this man are unfounded and a disgrace. I would like to personally apologize to Mr. Wilson for having him here today."

The chairman thought of the senator from Tennessee and said, "I think just about everybody here in this chamber agree with you, Senator. I would also like to apologize to Mr. Wilson and thank him for coming here today. I order this hearing to be dismissed." The chairman hit the gobble down on the table, and the senate was adjourned. Everybody started leaving the chamber, and Rusty got up and told William and Larry, "Let's go home." As soon as Rusty got home, Kathy asked him how everything went.

"Everything is fine now, princess. Let's go to the cabin and spend a few days and forget all about this."

After spending a few days at the cabin, Rusty and Kathy returned home. The next day, Rusty returned to his office. He called William and Larry to come to his office. When Larry and William arrived at Rusty's office, he said, "This is what I want you to do. I want you to form a group of investigators and start investigating any and all politicians that you may think are breaking the laws of this state. We also may go nationwide with our investigation. It's time we put some of these corrupt politicians out of business."

"We will get right on it, Rusty. I'll put together the best investigation group there are."

Rusty said, "It sounds good so let me get to work too."

After several months of investigation, a lot of the politicians began resigning their jobs.

They were afraid Rusty's investigations would wind up putting them in jail. Politicians, not only in Tennessee but also all over the country, started getting worried about Rusty's investigations. The director of the FBI called Rusty one day and told him that a lot of politicians were beginning to get worried about his investigations.

"You could be stepping on a lot of toes, Rusty, so make sure you watch your backside."

Rusty thanked the director for his concerns and told him he would be very careful.

Chapter 15

After several years, Rusty's investigating politicians brought an end to a lot of the corruption in the country. Rusty received a lot of threats while investigating and had to have special teams of bodyguards surrounding him and his company. Rusty told Kathy, "All the projects I have started are now completed. The resort area can now be enjoyed by all the employees. I'm going to call a special meeting with all the departments."

The next day, Rusty met with all the heads of the departments and told them he was planning to retire. He and Kathy were going to do a lot of traveling, and they would be running the company. "I'm turning the construction company over to Mark and Jesse. Bill Roberts will be taking over the law firm. Sally Rivers will be taking over the banking, and Tommy Johns will be running the engineering department. James Walker will be heading all the small businesses. The ranch in Australia and the resort in Nevada will be run by William Clark and Larry Cork. Starting tomorrow, everything this company owns will be in your hands. If you ever have problems, I will be as close as the phone. We will be coming back on occasions to spend time in the cabin and visit with all of you. I wish all of you the best of luck, and take care of our businesses."

The meeting was over, and everyone went back to their office and started running the business like Rusty wanted them to do. The next day, Rusty and Kathy gathered their luggage and headed for the airport. Rusty had his own private plane, and they would be doing most of their traveling in it. As the years went by, they traveled all over the world. Every year or so, Rusty and Kathy would return to

Indian Springs and spend time in their home and in the cabin. After a few weeks, they would be off again and flying all over the country to other places. Rusty and Kathy were enjoying the greatest love story anyone could ever want to talk about. They both had everything they ever dreamed for. While vacationing in Florida, Rusty received a phone call that would break his heart. Jesse and his wife had been killed in a plane crash.

"Kathy, pack everything. We've got to fly to Texas."

"I thought we were staying in Florida for another week, Rusty?"

"I just got a phone call from Mark. His brother Jesse and his wife have been killed in a plane crash just south of Port Arthur, Texas. I told Mark we would meet him in Port Arthur at the airport."

"Oh, Rusty, I'm so sorry. I know Jesse meant a lot to you."

"Jesse was like a brother to me. I've got to get out there and find out what happened."

Kathy and Rusty packed up in a hurry and headed to the airport. They boarded Rusty's private plane and flew straight to Texas. When they got to Port Arthur Airport, Mark was there, waiting on them. Rusty embraced Mark and told him how much he hated to hear the bad news about Jesse. "You know you and Jesse are two of the closest persons I have in my world."

"I know, Rusty. I feel the same about you."

"Tell me, Mark, what has happened?"

"All I can tell you, Rusty, is the airport authorities told me that Jesse was circling the airfield and crash-landed about a half a mile away. Jesse's and his wife's bodies were sent to the morgue. The FAA is investigating the crash right now. I hope you don't mind, Rusty, but I call William down here to do our own investigation."

"Well, that's what I was going to suggest. I would like our own people to investigate this. When I left Florida, all I could think about was, did someone do this to get even with me?"

"No, Rusty, I don't think that's the case here. If it is, I promise you we will find out!"

Rusty asked Kathy, "Go to the airport, and get us a room. Mark and I are going out to the crash site. I'm not sure how long we'll be out there, but I'll call you and let you know as soon as we head back."

After all the investigation, Mark and Rusty arrived at the crash site. There was a large group of investigators looking at the crash site. Rusty told the man in charge of the investigation that he had his own investigator coming down to help investigate.

"That's good, Mr. Wilson. We could use all the help we could get."

After about three hours, William showed up. William told Mark how sorry he was to hear about his brother and that he would do all he could to find out what happened. Rusty and Mark headed back to the airport hotel and were waiting to hear more about what had happened. After three days of investigating the crash, they determined the crash was caused by faulty wiring. After the investigation was over, Mark flew his brother and his wife back to Indian Springs, where they would be buried. It was a sad day for Indian Springs when they had the funeral for Jesse and his wife. Rusty went home that night after the funeral. He sat there in his chair by the fireplace and cried. He told Kathy, "This is one of the saddest days in my life. It seems like everybody I'm close to, bad things seem to happen."

"I know how you feel, Rusty. You can't blame yourself for this. We have each other to hold on to at times like this."

"I know, princess. I still have you, and that's all that matters."

Several years passed after Jesse's death. Rusty and Kathy got back to their same old routine and were enjoying life once again.

Chapter 16

Rusty and Kathy were spending time in Savannah, Georgia, when Rusty got a phone call from William.

"Rusty, I wanted to call you and let you know, Bob has been released from prison."

"That can't be true, William. He hasn't served his forty years yet."

"He went before the parole board, Rusty, and they released him. I found out as soon as he was released where he went. He went back to Alabama."

"Well, I'm not really worried about it, William. I don't think he will cause us any problems."

"Okay, Rusty. If you need me, let me know."

"Thank you, William. I appreciate you letting me know that."

Later on that afternoon, Rusty was trying to decide if he should tell Kathy. That night, after dinner, Rusty told Kathy that Bob had been released.

"Do you think he's going to cause us any problems, Rusty?"

"No, princess, I don't think he's going to be coming around us. So let's just enjoy the rest of our trip."

Rusty and Kathy spent several weeks in Savannah and then decided to fly back home. They spent several days in their house and then decided to go up to the cabin. The first night at the cabin, Rusty told Kathy, "This cabin is probably my most special place in the world. I think the princess and I may have been reborn here."

"What do you mean, Rusty? Reborn?"

"Well, when Bob shot me up here and the two doctors found me and saved my life, it changed me more than you will ever know.

I made a promise that I would do everything in my life to make this world a better place to live, and I think I have done that. The two men that saved my life, I have never seen again and don't even know where they are now."

"Rusty, I'm glad they saved your life because you saved my life. You are the most important thing in my life, and I don't know what I would do without you."

"I feel the same way about you, princess. I would be lost without you."

They were sitting in front of the fireplace, reminiscing and talking about the good times they we're having.

"Rusty, you have made my life a dream come true, and I will always love you."

"Princess, I think I will go out to the car and get my guitar. I will sing you a song."

"Do that, Rusty. I love to hear you sing."

Rusty got up and walked out the door to get his guitar, and all of a sudden, there was a gunshot. Rusty fell to the floor of the porch. Kathy heard the shot and went outside to see what had happened. She saw Rusty lying on the floor with a gunshot to his head. She screamed, "Oh, God, no," and grabbed Rusty and held him in her arms.

A few minutes later, Gus walked up and said, "I was at the burial site and I heard a gunshot. I saw a car speeding away and decided to come down here and see what was going on."

"Rusty's been shot. Gus, help me get him to the hospital."

Kathy and Gus picked Rusty up and put him in the car and headed down the mountain to the hospital. Kathy called the hospital and told them she was on her way there with Rusty, and he had been shot. "Please have everyone there to help me when I get there."

It took about thirty minutes to get to the hospital. They carried Rusty into the emergency room and started trying to save his life. They worked on Rusty for about thirty minutes, but there was no way they could save his life. The wounds to the head were too massive, and there was nothing they could do. Kathy waited outside while the doctors were working on Rusty. Finally, one of the doctors walked out and told Kathy there was nothing they could do for him. Kathy screamed and said, "Where is he? I want to see him."

The doctors took Kathy back into the emergency room were Rusty was lying. Kathy bent down and held Rusty, crying and kept telling him how much she loved him. The doctors told Kathy she should go and wait outside until the authorities could get there, and she could tell them what happened. The police arrived a few minutes later and started asking Kathy all kinds of questions about what happened and where it happened. She told them they were at the cabin, and someone shot Rusty when he went outside to get his guitar.

She told them, when she heard the shot, she ran outside, and there was no one to be seen until Gus showed up. The police questioned Gus for about thirty minutes, and he told them all he knew. Mark was notified and told to come to the police station.

Mark arrived at the police station, and they told him that Rusty had been shot and killed and was asked if he knew anybody that might have wanted him dead. Mark told the police, "The only person I know that might want to do that would be Bob."

Kathy's ex-husband was the prime suspect, and everybody started looking for him. Mark left the police station and went to the hospital where Kathy was. Kathy was screaming to Mark, "No, this can't be true. This can't be happening."

Mark put his arms around her and told her, "We'll find out who did this. I promise you."

Kathy was so upset; she could barely stand. Mark said, "Let me take you home, Kathy, and I'll get somebody to stay with you."

Mark took Kathy home and called Sally to come stay with her until he could get a nurse there. Sally showed up and told Mark she would stay with her for the rest of the night. Sally tried talking to Kathy, but she would not speak. She sat there in shock and didn't say anything. Soon the nurse showed up and told Sally she would give Kathy a sedative, and that would help her rest. The nurse carried Kathy into the bedroom and put her in bed. She told Sally that she'd be fine until the morning. Sally and the nurse stayed with Kathy all night. The next morning, Mark showed up and told Sally, "I'm having security guards all the way around the house until we find out who did this."

Sally asked Mark, "Who could have done this, Mark?"

"I don't know, but I'm sure I'm going to try and find out."

The next day, Bob Ford was picked up and questioned for several hours. Bob had a good witness to prove he was nowhere near Indian Springs when Rusty was shot. the police said they didn't have enough evidence, and they really didn't think Bob had done this shooting. All the police agencies were searching for evidence in the mountain.

The next day, the nurse told Sally someone else would have to make all the arrangements for Rusty's burial. She said Kathy was not going to be able to do anything. "She's in a state of shock right now, and all we can do is watch after her."

Mark came by, and Sally told him what the nurse said about making the arrangements. Mark said, "I will do all that we just have to take care of Kathy right now."

The next two days, Mark made all the arrangements to have Rusty buried next to his parents. They were going to have the funeral at the church the next day. Mark and Sally went to get Kathy and took her to the church. After everything was over at the church, they went to the cemetery where Rusty would be buried. The cemetery was so crowded that day with all the people. No one could get within a quarter of a mile to the cemetery. The funeral lasted for an hour at the grave site. The bagpipes were playing, and there was not a dry eye at the cemetery. There was a strange sound coming from the mountain, and everyone turned to look that way. Sally asked Mark, "Did you hear that sound coming from the mountain?"

"Yes, I did, Sally."

They started lowering Rusty to the ground, and Kathy collapsed. Mark and Sally grabbed her and carried her to the car they came to the cemetery in. Mark told Sally, "We're going to have to have somebody to stay with her for a while. We'll get nurses to stay with her around the clock until she gets better."

They carried Kathy home and put her in bed and told her they would be back the next day to check on her. "There'll be somebody here with you all the time, and you don't have to worry about anything."

Kathy sat there and did not make a sound. She was lost in her own little world. The search for Rusty's killer was still going on. After several weeks, Kathy sat and talked with Mark and Sally. Mark told Kathy everything. "The business is going good. And as soon as you're able, we would like for you to come back to the office."

"I'm not ready for that, Mark. But when I am, I will let you know."

One day, Kathy was sitting on the front porch in Rusty's grandfather's rocking chair.

A car drove up out front, and it was Seth Adams. Seth got out of his car and walked over to the gate, and the security guard asked him, "What are you doing here, and who are you?"

"My name is Seth Adams. I'm a newspaper writer, and I was writing a story about Rusty when I heard about what happened to him. I would like to talk to his wife if she will let me."

The security guard said, "Wait right here, and I'll go up and ask her."

The security guard returned and said, "She will talk to you for a few minutes, and then you'll have to leave."

"Thank you, sir," and Seth started walking up the sidewalk to the front porch.

"Ms. Wilson, my name is Seth Adams. I'm a newspaper writer from Memphis, Tennessee. I've been talking to a good friend of Rusty's. Her name is Becky, and she was telling me all about Rusty. I'm sorry I never got to meet him, but I would like to finish my story that I am writing about him. There are just a few things that I would like to ask you, if you don't mind."

"What is it you want to know about my husband?"

"I have talked to a lot of people about Rusty, but I want to hear from you what kind of man he was."

"He was a loving man. He loved everybody and wanted to do good for the entire world. He loved me more than anybody ever has. I don't think there has ever been a man in this world that was as good as he was. I will miss him more than anyone will ever know. I think

THE LEGEND OF DOGWOOD MOUNTAIN

maybe he is still alive somewhere in the mountains. That's all I have to say, Mr. Adams."

"Thank you, Ms. Wilson, for your time. I plan to share the world with his story." Seth turned around and walked away. When he got to his car and started to drive away, he looked back and said, "That is one beautiful woman. She is definitely a princess."

Mark came by the next day and asked Kathy, "Are you about ready to go back to work?"

She said, "Yes, Mark, I think I may come back the first of next week. I'm thinking maybe I'll go up to the cabin and spend a few days before I come back to work."

"Do you want somebody to go up to the cabin with you?"

"No, Mark, I want to be by myself. I'll be all right, and I'll keep in touch with you."

"Okay, Kathy. You make sure you call me and let me know how things are going up there."

"I will."

Kathy got up and walked back into her house. Mark left and told the security guard, "Let me know when she leaves."

The next day, Kathy left for the mountains. She called Mark and told him she was at the cabin, and she would be back to work Monday morning. Mark said, "Call me, and let me know everything's okay."

"I'll keep in touch with you, Mark. Don't worry about me."

Mark waited all weekend for Kathy to call him, but she never did call. He began to get worried, and he told Sally he might drive up to the mountains.

Sally said, "Why don't you wait till Monday morning and go by her house and pick her up and bring her to work?"

"Well, maybe you're right I'll wait till Monday."

Monday morning came, and Kathy was nowhere to be found. Mark said to the security guard, "I'm going up to the mountain." Mark got in his car and headed to the mountain.

When Mark arrived at the cabin, there was no sign of Kathy anywhere. Her car was sitting there, and her cell phone was lying in the front seat. He walked inside the cabin, and her purse was lying on the couch. There was no sign of Kathy anywhere. He decided to walk up to the burial grounds to see if she might have been up there. When he got there, Gus was sitting on the bench inside the burial site. Mark said, "I'm looking for Kathy. Have you seen her?"

"Yes, I saw her sitting right here on this bench last night. I told her to make sure she locked the gate when she left. When I got back down here this morning, the gate was still open, and I didn't see her anywhere."

"What was she doing when you saw her sitting on the bench?"

"Well, when I first walked up, she was sitting there, crying, and I asked her if there was anything I could do for her. She said, 'No, I'm just missing my husband.' We talked for a while, and I left."

Mark said, "Don't go anywhere. I'm going to call the authorities to come up here and help me find her."

Mark called the sheriff's department and told them Kathy was missing and to get all the help he could to help find her. It didn't take long. The mountain was covered with people looking for Kathy. They looked all over the mountain that day and found no sign of her. The FBI was called in, and they were thinking she had been kidnapped. Mark said, "Maybe the same people that shot Rusty had kidnapped Kathy."

Their search went on all day up until it got dark. They called the search off and returned the next morning to continue the search. They searched the mountain for three days, and there was no sign of Kathy, no evidence where she had gone. They finally called the search off in the mountain and started looking everywhere else where she might be.

Seth Adams was back in Memphis, writing his story about Rusty, when he heard Kathy had disappeared. He told everybody at the newspaper he was going to Indian Springs to help find her. When he arrived in Indian Springs, he called Mark to find out if it was okay for him to go up to the cabin. Mark said, "Why do you want to go to the cabin?"

Seth answered, "I really don't know. It's just a feeling I have. I just feel like I need to go up there and look for her."

"I guess it'll be okay, Seth, but you need to make sure it's okay with the sheriff's department."

Seth got the okay from the sheriff's department. He was on his way to the cabin in the mountains when he passed by the Indian burial site and saw Gus standing by the gate. He stopped and walked down to the site, and he asked Gus who he was. "My name is Gus, and I'm the caretaker of this burial site. Who are you, sir?"

"My name is Seth Adams. I'm a newspaper writer, and I've been writing a story about Rusty Wilson when I heard about Kathy disappearing. Is there anything you can tell me about her?"

"Well, the last time I saw Mrs. Wilson, she was sitting on that bench, crying. I walked up and asked if I could help her, and she said she was waiting on Rusty. She said she heard his voice calling to her, and she was going to stay there until he got there. I asked her how she knew he was calling her, and she said he told her that she was the only love of his life and called her princess. 'He's the only person that ever calls me princess. I know that was him,' and she was sitting here, waiting on him."

"So where do you think she is, Gus?"

"I think she's with the spirits right now, but she'll be back."

"Well, I'm going down to the cabin and look around, and I will talk to you again, Gus."

Seth left and walked down to the cabin. He just sat there at the cabin, trying to figure out what Gus was talking about. Gus seemed like he knew more than what he was telling, so he was going to stick around for a while. He was walking around in the front yard, and he walked over to the edge of the mountainside. It was getting dark, and he looked down the edge of the mountain and thought he saw a light. The light looked like it was coming out of the side of the mountain, so he decided to climb down the mountainside.

When he got down to where the light was shining through, there was a small opening in the side of the mountain. He walked through the opening, and he could see a big opening inside the mountain. All of a sudden, he could see someone sitting on a small bench. It was Kathy Wilson sitting there with a smile on her face. He walked up to her and said, "Ms. Wilson, everybody has been looking for you. Are you okay?"

"Yes, I am fine."

"What are you doing here?"

"I've been here with my husband. He just left. He said everything is okay now. You can go home. Will you take me home?"

"Yes, I will, Ms. Wilson. I will be proud to take you home."

Seth carried Ms. Wilson home. When she got there, the security guard asked her, where she had been.

"I will tell everybody later where I've been right now, I want to go in and get some sleep."

Seth walked her up to the front door and told her he would be back tomorrow morning to make sure she was okay.

"Thank you, Seth. I will see you in the morning."

The next morning, Seth called Mark and told him Kathy was at home. Mark didn't hesitate for a second as he was on his way to Kathy's house.

Before Mark arrived, Kathy was standing on the front porch, dressed and ready to go to work. When Mark pulled up in front of the house, Kathy was walking down the sidewalk to the gate. Mark got out of his car, walked up to Kathy, and said, "Where have you been? Everybody's been worried about you."

"I'm okay, Mark. Everything is well now. Let's go to work."

Mark walked out to his car, put Kathy in the car, turned, and looked at Seth, and walked back up to him.

"You brought her home. Where has she been?"

Seth looked at Mark with a big smile on his face and said, "She's been with the legend of Dogwood Mountain."

Seth turned and walked toward his car, got in, and drove away. Seth went back to Memphis and finished writing his story about Rusty Wilson. At the end of his story, he said, "All is well in Indian Springs."

The End

I hope everyone enjoys reading this book as much as I have enjoyed writing it.

—John D. Garrison, author

About the Author

He was born John Dewey Garrison and grew up on a mini farm. They lived on the outskirts of Adamsville, Alabama. He had five brothers and seven sisters growing up, and he was number seven. The family was blessed to have had their dad and mom together for sixty-three years. His dad taught the older sons carpentry skills. One of the elder brothers taught him. His brother helped him get his first job with a construction company. He worked in construction for many years and made a good living. He also worked as a maintenance supervisor for many years. He has now given up his hammer and picked up a pen to start a new adventure writing stories.